"I'm going to keep my
promise..."

"The first time—your first time—I was an anxious
kid..." He drew in a deep breath. "And my first
night back in town, I was drunk. Both times I was
thinking about me, Annie. About how you made me
feel, how desperate I was to be inside you. But I
want to make *you* feel this time. That's all I've been
thinking about. How I'd touch you, what I'd do...."

"So stop talking and do it," Annie said impishly.

He grinned, then touched his lips to hers, so light
and teasing she groaned. Then he licked a path
down her neck, gradually sliding lower. Her fingers
threaded through his hair, holding him to her breast
as he suckled her until she writhed beneath him, her
hips moving, begging for more. *For him.*

He nibbled a path down the warm skin of her belly.
"Ah, honey, you feel so good. So hot and wet... Just
the way I want you." His fingertips trailed over the
insides of her thighs. When he touched her with his
mouth, she started, then gradually spread her legs
wider, giving him better access to the sweetness
inside.

Tack didn't count on the fierce wave of
possessiveness that swept through him at that
moment. The sudden desperate urge to brand every
inch of her as his, to touch her in ways no man ever
could. Because Annie Divine was his...whether she
admitted it or not.

Dear Reader,

I love bad boys! There's just something about a wicked, charming, dangerously handsome man who's too big for his britches that really gets my blood pumping. It's no wonder I fell hard and fast when Tack Brandon walked into my mind, teasing and flirting, daring me to find him a woman strong enough, passionate enough, to tame him.

Well, as you can see, I couldn't resist the *Temptation,* so to speak. In *Breathless,* Tack returns home to Inspiration, Texas, to lay his past to rest. The girl he left behind, Annie Divine, is all grown-up now, and she's determined to resist falling in love with such a heartbreaker again.

Neither count on the fierce and explosive passion that ignites between them. A passion that has nothing to do with the sweltering Texas heat and everything to do with the past, the present and the one *Breathless* night spent in each other's arms.

I'm thrilled that this story is part of the Blaze series! Life is real, and so is the love, both physical and emotional, that bonds man and woman together. Being true to my characters, portraying their passion in love as well as life, is my strongest desire as a writer, and Blaze gives me the freedom to do just that!

So grab something cold to drink, turn up the air conditioner and get ready for a five-alarm read!

Kimberly Raye

P.S. I'd love to know what you think about my first Temptation novel. Write to me: c/o Harlequin Books, 225 Duncan Mill Road, Don Mills, Ontario, M3B 3K9, Canada.

BREATHLESS
Kimberly Raye

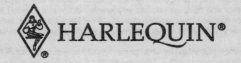

TORONTO • NEW YORK • LONDON
AMSTERDAM • PARIS • SYDNEY • HAMBURG
STOCKHOLM • ATHENS • TOKYO • MILAN • MADRID
PRAGUE • WARSAW • BUDAPEST • AUCKLAND

For my oldest and dearest friend,
Liz Eden Kasper.
For great memories and a timeless friendship.
You're the best!

ISBN 0-373-25828-3

BREATHLESS

1

SHE KNEW HIM immediately.

A girl didn't forget the first man she'd ever made love to—the *only* man—even if it had been ten years ago.

He sat several feet away at a small table near the center of BJ's, the town's only honky-tonk. With his legs propped up, arms folded and eyes closed, it appeared that he'd stretched out and fallen asleep, despite the fast-paced George Strait song blaring from the speakers.

She moved forward and made her way through a maze of tables. It seemed as if the entire population of Inspiration, Texas, filled the small place. Then again, it was Friday night. Time to let down your hair and kick up your spurs. The tables were jam-packed, the dance floor to her left full of sliding boots and wiggling Wranglers.

She saw more than one familiar face as she scooted past this chair and squeezed by that one, not that anyone acknowledged her. The women either stared past her as if she didn't exist, or shot her a look of pure contempt. And the men... Open, hungry stares without an ounce of respect roved over her and picked her clean.

Annie Divine didn't shy away or wince or show any of the dozen emotions whirling through her. Shoulders back, head held high, she kept walking.

The country two-step ended just as she reached him. The sudden pause magnified every sound around her. The spurts of laughter. The murmur of conversation. The *clink* of beer bottles. The *ding* of a pinball machine. Her heart echoed in her ears, pounding out a furious tempo that betrayed the composure she was trying so hard to maintain.

As if it even mattered.

Tack Brandon was drunk, maybe passed out, from the looks of him. Definitely passed out, she corrected when a nearby pool player hit an eight ball. A round of cheers erupted and the next song started with a loud guitar riff, but Tack didn't so much as flinch. He simply sat there, completely unaffected by his surroundings, by her.

The realization eased the panic beating at her senses, and she took a deep breath. The moment held a sudden surreal quality, as if she wasn't really living and breathing the here and now, but imagining it. She would open her eyes soon and find that this was all a dream. Cooper Brandon, Tack's father, would be alive and well and Tack would be anywhere but here. Anywhere but *home*. The thought filled her with an overwhelming sadness and she found herself holding her breath, holding the moment. He was here. Now. Right in front of her.

She almost didn't believe it. When he hadn't shown up for his father's funeral earlier that day, she'd started to wonder if he really did hate Cooper Brandon as much as he'd claimed. The question had weighed heavy on her, filling her with a mix of relief and despair. Both ridiculous, considering she shouldn't care if she ever saw Tack again.

She shouldn't, but she did.

The prodigal son was home.

Only he hadn't come home. He'd come here, she thought, her gaze going to a blazing neon Coors sign. A place to drown his troubles. To find trouble, if he had a mind. And from the stories Coop had told her over the past few years, Tack certainly had a hankering for that.

"How're you holding up, sugar?"

A warm hand closed over Annie's shoulder and she turned to see Bobby Jack, the club's owner, standing next to her.

She shrugged. "A little tired. Today was more difficult than I expected."

"Sorry I had to add to your troubles and drag you out of bed, but I didn't know who to call. I figured you was the closest thing to family Tack's got now. I been pouring coffee in him for the past hour, but he still ain't fit to drive."

"I couldn't sleep anyway." Or eat. Or breathe easily. She blinked. "I can't believe he's really here."

Bobby Jack gave her shoulder a reassuring squeeze. He stood a few inches shy of Annie's five-nine, but what he lacked in height, he made up in brawn. Built like a pit bull, he had a face only his mama and Norma Jean Mayberry, his fiancé, could love. His nose, a little too wide and flat, gave the impression he'd taken one too many punches. Then there was the bruise darkening the left side of his face...

He noticed the direction of her gaze and shrugged. "When the coffee didn't work, I tried a pitcher of ice water over his head. It always does the trick for Dell Carter. That old drunk comes up sputtering sober every time."

"But Tack came up punching?"

"Knocked me clear across the dance floor before he sank back into his chair and reached for another drink." Bobby rubbed his jaw. "Boy's got damn fine aim considering he guzzled close to a full bottle of tequila." He handed her a pair of keys. "I wrestled these off him a few minutes ago. Belong to that big bitch of a motorcycle parked out front..." His words died as someone motioned to him from a nearby table.

"Looks like I've got customers."

"You go on. I can manage."

"I'll be back to help you as soon as I can." Instead of rushing away, however, Bobby Jack paused. "I didn't get a chance to tell you at the funeral, but I'm real sorry about Coop. He was a good man." He shook his head. "Never thought I'd say that about him."

"It's all right, Bobby Jack. Coop knew he wasn't in the running for any popularity contests."

"Ain't that the God's honest. He was always a hard-assed SOB, but these past few years he seemed to soften up." He squeezed her shoulder again. "You did good, Annie. Your mama woulda been real proud." Then, as if he'd said too much, he pulled his hand away. "You need anything, anything at all, you let me know."

His concern touched her and she slid her arms around his wide shoulders for a quick hug. Bobby Jack had always been one of the few in town who treated Annie like a person, a friend, and not Wild Cherry Divine's daughter.

Not that her parentage bothered her. Annie had long ago come to terms with who she was. The moment Tack Brandon had roared out of town, and out of her life.

"Thanks, Bobby Jack." She gave him another quick hug before pulling away, Tack's keys clutched in her hand.

"*Anything*," Bobby said again.

She nodded and watched him disappear into a cloud of cigarette smoke, then she turned back to the matter at hand.

To him.

If only she'd brought her camera, she thought as she stole the next few heartbeats just to look at and appreciate the changes ten years had wrought. Time had turned the gangly teenage boy into a hard and muscular man. His white T-shirt—soaking-wet from Bobby Jack's douse of ice water—clung to his sinewy torso like a second skin, revealing a solid chest, a ridged abdomen. Her gaze lingered at the shadow of a nipple beneath the transparent material, and a dozen erotic memories rushed through her.

Her lips closing over the flat button, tongue flicking the bud to life. His deep, throaty groan echoing in her ears, his hands buried in her hair, urging her on...

She took a deep breath and moved her attention to the damp jeans molded to his thighs, his calves. Scuffed black biker boots completed the outfit. His entire persona screamed *danger*. Tack Brandon was a womanizer, a use-'em-then-lose-'em type with a taste for sin and a body to back him up. He was the sort of man every mama warned her daughter about.

Every mama except Annie's. But how could Cherry have warned her daughter off the very type she herself had spent a lifetime trying to catch? The woman had been a lot of things, but never a hypocrite. She'd been loud and a bit gaudy, quick to rile and even quicker to forgive, naive in so many ways, yet experienced to the point of being the town Jezebel. Trustworthy and too easy to place her own trust, and loyal to a fault. Cherry Divine had given up her hopes and dreams and gone to her grave loving Cooper Brandon even though he'd never loved her back. Not the way he should have.

Like father, like son.

In appearance as well as deed, she thought, her gaze going to Tack's face. He had his father's features, the strong Brandon cheekbones inherited from a Comanche grandmother, as well as a straight, sculpted nose. Obscenely long sable eyelashes fanned his cheeks. A few days' growth of beard covered his jaw, crept down his neck. His brown hair, as damp as his shirt, curled down around his neck, the edges highlighted the same gold as the inch of tequila left in the bottle sitting in front of him.

Her palms burned as she remembered the softness of his hair—velvet strands stroking her breasts, trailing over her navel, brushing the insides of her thighs... Heat flamed her cheeks and she said a silent thank-you to the heavens and Cuervo Gold that his eyes were closed.

The fire cooled with several deep breaths and she continued her inspection. Tiny lines fanned out from the corners of his eyes. A scar zigzagged from his right temple and bisected one dark eyebrow. The subtle changes made him seem much older than the boy of eighteen who haunted her memories.

This was no boy. He was all man, and he had the hard look of someone who'd seen too much, spent the better part of his life sacrificing and doing without.

Ridiculous, she knew. Tack Brandon had never done without anything. He'd had everything he'd ever wanted, including her. Then again, he'd never *really* wanted her, not the way she'd wanted him.

Thankfully.

She focused on the thought and tried to restrain the emotions swirling inside her. To ignore the memory of his body covering hers, his hands stroking her bare skin, his tears wetting her palms... She didn't want to remember the way his touch had set her senses blazing. The way his gaze, usually so guarded and emotionless, had gleamed with raw feeling for those few moments when she'd been in his arms and he'd been inside of her.

The past was over and done with. She wasn't going to fall in love with him again, she told herself for the hundredth time that day. She *wasn't*.

The trouble was, Annie Divine didn't think she'd ever fallen out of love with Tack Brandon.

And when his eyelids fluttered and he stared up
at her with a gaze as blue and enticing as a clear
midnight sky, she feared she hadn't.

Like mother, like daughter.

Tack Brandon hadn't taken just her innocence
the night of their senior prom, the night his
mother had died and he'd left Inspiration. He'd
taken her heart, as well.

No. The past was over and done with and Annie had learned her lesson where he was concerned. Never again.

"Hey there, sweetheart."

He sounded more sober than drunk, but his
gaze, red-rimmed and glazed, told a different
story. Then there was his smile, a wicked tilt to
his lips that stopped her heart for several long
seconds. Definitely drunk, she thought. Because
the last thing Tack would offer her would be a
smile. His boot up her backside maybe, once he
realized she'd befriended the one man he'd always hated. A man she'd hated herself up until
the moment her mama had passed away. Things
had changed then. Cooper Brandon had changed.

She made a point of keeping her fanny aimed
away from Tack as she scooted around and
worked her hand beneath one heavily muscled
arm.

"Come on, cowboy. Let's get you home."

Her words seemed to trigger something and
his smile died. "To hell with that. Motel," he
mumbled, and she noticed the room key sitting
on the table next to his wallet and the tequila bottle. He must have emptied his pockets digging for
money to pay for his liquor, she thought, scoop-

ing up his possessions and aiming for her own pocket.

His hand clamped around her wrist and she found herself jerked onto his lap, his face inches from hers.

"Take it easy," she told him. "I'm just going to hold on to this stuff for you while I get you out of here."

"You pickin' me up, sugar?" He smiled again. "This must be my lucky night." His breath, a mingling of lime and tequila and a sweetness she remembered all too well, rushed softly against her mouth. Then his lips were there, nibbling at the corners of hers. "Best luck I've had in a hell of a long time."

Her mind replayed a dozen memories and it was all she could do to turn her head to the side and keep from meeting his kiss.

"I'm just helping you back to your room. You're drunk."

"And you're..." He leaned back and squinted, as if he couldn't quite see through the liquor fogging his senses. "Do I know you?"

"Maybe," she said, doing her best to ignore the pang of hurt that shot through her at the simple question.

Calm.

She pushed herself up off his lap, her hand plastered against the rock-hard wall of his chest. Her palm caught fire from the simple contact and she nearly cried. It wasn't fair that his effect on her should be so potent, so powerful after all this time.

Cool.

He grabbed for her again, but she sidestepped him. "Come on," she said, sliding a hand under one large bicep and urging him from the chair.

It took her several tugs, but finally she managed to get him on his feet. She slid an arm around his waist and six-feet-plus of warm male leaned into her.

"What's your name, sugar?" he drawled, his voice as lazy and thick as molasses.

"Sugar's, fine." She ignored the prick at her ego, her heart, and concentrated on holding him up and urging him forward.

Indifferent.

"I swear," he slurred, "I...know you...from somewhere." He shook his head. "You an old girlfriend, sugar?" He didn't give her a chance to reply. "You are. I knew it!" He slapped his knee, the motion making them both stumble. She caught the edge of the table and he sagged against her. "A blast from the past," he mumbled.

"That's me. Now, hut-two, cowboy." She motioned for Bobby Jack who'd just served up a round to a nearby table. At five-nine, Annie towered over most of the women she knew, as well as a few men, but Tack was still a good head taller and she needed all the help she could get. "Let's see about drying you off and putting you to bed."

"Bed," he muttered, his head dropping onto her shoulder, his lips nibbling at the curve of her neck. "Now, there's a fine idea."

HE'D HAD THE DREAM many times.

She leaned over him, her pale hair falling down around her face like a shimmering curtain of silvery silk that tickled across his belly as she worked at the button of his jeans.

"Just my luck Bobby had to pour ice water over him," a soft, sweet voice grumbled from someplace far, far away, "...my even worse luck it's colder than Iceland in here...should've let Bobby follow me...but no, I had to tell him I could handle it." He heard a few more mutters about motel air conditioners and pneumonia before her fingers slipped and grazed Tack's already growing erection. His heartbeat thundered through his head.

Again she tried to work the zipper, and instead, worked him into a frenzy. Every muscle in his body went tense, his breathing grew heavy, labored. He sucked for a deep breath.

Through the haze of tequila and smoke that hovered around him, he caught a whiff of her—the tantalizing smell of ripe peaches basking in the summer sunshine.

He drank in the scent, his nostrils flaring, his senses coming alive as her essence pushed aside the liquor-induced fog, to coax him back to life. Peaches had always been his favorite. He remembered so many warm days picking fruit down by Brandon Creek. There'd been nothing like biting into the sweet flesh, feeling the juice trickle down his chin...

Nothing as decadent, as satisfying.

Except her—the woman who haunted his past, his dreams, his *now*—and her soft-as-moonlight hair that whispered across his bare flesh and made his muscles quiver.

His zipper slid completely free. She sighed and

he groaned, and then he reached for her, anxious for the part of the fantasy that came next.

He laced his fingers through the smooth strands of her hair and pulled her down on top of him.

A surprised "Oh!" bubbled from her lips before he claimed them in a kiss that was desperate, savage. He'd been far too long without a woman.

Without *this* woman.

Full, soft lips pressed against his. She drew back with a moment's hesitation that barely registered in his brain, then her mouth parted for him and her tongue flicked out to stroke his. He held her head in his hands, his fingers tangled in her hair, anchoring her to him as if he feared someone might pull her away.

Hell, he was afraid. He knew from experience he would wake up all too soon to find his bed empty and his body spent on another wet dream.

But at the moment, she felt like much more. *So real.* The sound of her shallow breaths filled his ears. Her hands trailed up his arms, over his shoulders, silky fingertips touching and stroking as if memorizing every inch of him. Her heart pounded against his. Her nipples swelled, pebbled against the thin cotton of her T-shirt. Her hips rotated, echoing the same desperate urgency clawing his belly.

Just a dream...

The best he'd had in a hell of a long time.

Clothes were peeled away, from her shirt and jeans and wispy panties, to what was left of his. He urged her up, sliding her sweat-dampened body along the aching length of his until her nipple hovered a fraction from his lips. He drew the quivering tip into his mouth and suckled her long and hard, until she was gasping and crying out his name.

He savored the sound of her response before he moved on to the other breast. He suckled and nipped until she bucked against him, so wild and untamed. The way she'd been their first night together, once she'd shed that damn potato sack of a dress. He'd peeled away the fabric with gentle kisses and heated words, and along with her clothing, he'd finally managed to strip her of her inhibitions, as well. She'd matched his appetite, his eagerness, just the way she did right now. The way she always did when he had this particular dream.

He was near to bursting, his sex hot and heavy and pulsing with a life all its own. Gliding his hands down her back, he cupped her buttocks and lifted her. With a shift of his hips, he touched her with the tip of his erection, felt her warm and wet and waiting for him. His fingers tightened on her firm bottom and in one smooth motion he slid her down his rigid length. Pleasure splintered his brain and sent an echoing shudder through his body. He gripped her hips and urged her to move, to ride him fast and furious.

"Wait." So soft and desperate, the word echoed through his head and pushed aside the desire drumming through his veins to jerk him back to reality.

But this wasn't reality. This was a dream. A very vivid, erotic fanta—

A splash of wetness hit his cheek and he knew

in an instant that the woman in his arms was very real. His hands immediately stilled. He forced his eyes open, battling the damn fuzziness brought on by all the tequila.

He blinked and tried to focus, but the room was nearly pitch-black, so dark and blurry. He saw only the shadow of her face surrounded by a silver cloud of hair.

Her hair.

He forced the thought aside. It was a real woman, all right, but it couldn't be *her*. While the lights were out and lust clouded his brain, he saw what he wanted to see, felt what he wanted to feel, and man, she felt good!

Another splash hit his chin, slid down his jaw, and he raised a hand to wipe the wetness from her cheeks. He clamped down on his control, determined not to move, not to twitch inside her until he'd heard her answer. "I'm not hurting you, am I?"

"Yes. No." She sniffled. "I'm sorry. It's just been a long time." She drew a deep breath that ended on a ragged gasp when he reached up to thumb her nipple. "Too long," she added, leaning into his palm. "Much too long."

"Relax, darlin'." He stroked her back, felt her body bow toward him. "Just sit back and enjoy the ride."

At the coaxing of his hands, the slow, mesmerizing thrusts of his hips, she seemed to do just that. But not half as much as Tack, himself. When he came, it was like someone zapped his brain with a cattle prod. Heat sizzled across every nerve ending, consumed all rhyme and reason and thought, until he crashed and burned and his entire body went up in flames. And Tack Brandon had the second best orgasm of his entire life.

The first, of course, had been courtesy of the silver-haired beauty from his dreams. A memory.

A blast from the past.

The words echoed in his head, playing at his conscience, trying to remind him of something. But he was too tired, too spent, too pleased to think of anything except slipping an arm around this woman, *his* woman, nuzzling her neck and getting some much-needed sleep.

He'd have plenty of time to think tomorrow.

2

SHE WAS GONE.

Tack leaned up on one elbow and scanned the sparsely furnished motel room. With its orange shag carpeting and quarter-fed vibrating bed, the room, like all the others at the Inspiration Inn, served as home-away-from-home to truckers and eager lovers. Tack had considered himself neither when he'd signed the register yesterday. But now...

Visions of silky arms and long, long legs wrapped around him flashed in his mind. Heat skimmed over his bare flesh despite the air conditioner blasting ice-cold comfort from the wall unit not two feet away. *Eager.* That certainly described him last night. This morning, too, he thought ruefully, staring down at the portion of sheet raised in tentlike fashion over his prominent erection.

But his equally eager partner was nowhere in sight.

He took a deep breath and continued his visual search of the room. His wallet and keys sat atop a scarred dresser. His discarded clothes lay draped over the room's only chair, an orange vinyl number that made him want to reach for his sunglasses.

The rising sun didn't help matters any. A pale gold glow crept around the edges of the blinds to chase the shadows into the farthest corners. He clamped his eyes shut against the light as the first twinges of a major hangover needled his head. He was still sufficiently drunk that he didn't feel the full effect of the morning after, yet sober enough to recognize the hollowness in his gut.

She was really gone.

The dream was over.

But this hadn't been a dream. This had been a real woman, someone he'd picked up at BJ's. Maybe someone who'd picked him up. He searched his mind for a memory, but he couldn't grasp anything past Bobby Jack dumping that damn ice water on him. That and the crack of knuckles against his old friend's face. Tack had collapsed back into the chair, picked up the bottle again, and the world had faded away. The next thing he knew, he'd awakened to see all that angel hair trailing over his bare stomach.

His muscles shivered in response and he closed his eyes, feeling her over him, surrounding him, her body grasping him so perfectly. So warm and wet and—

What the hell had he done?

He wiped a hand over his face. He'd drunk himself into a stupor, that's what he'd done. Downed a full bottle of tequila when he never touched anything stronger than an occasional beer during off-season. While he raced the circuit, he stuck to sports drinks and bottled water. He *never* drank the hard stuff, any more than he slept with nameless, faceless women. Granted, he'd gone through his share of trophy girls when he'd started out, a rookie hotshot burning up the motocross tracks. Once he'd grown up, smartened up, he'd realized the women were just as bad for him as the booze. Distracting. Dangerous. He wasn't into one-night stands.

Then again, he hadn't really considered this woman a one-night stand. Just a dream. Another crazy fantasy. *The* fantasy that haunted him night after night.

But this had been real, with all too real repercussions. A dozen scenarios flashed in his head, all the result of unprotected sex. *If* it had been unprotected sex. Maybe she'd been on the Pill, or used a diaphragm or carried her own condoms. He clung to the hope and forced the doom and gloom aside. What was done was done, and Tack had never been one to linger over his mistakes. *Move on. Focus.*

Pushing himself up, he swung his legs over the side of the bed and spared a glance at the alarm clock. Half past seven and counting. Hangover be damned, he had to get dressed and get on with his business. Tucker was waiting for him—

The thought jerked to a halt as he remembered the sticky vinyl seat of a pickup truck, a woman's soft voice humming to a country tune playing on the radio. He went to the window, moved aside the blind and glanced out the window, squinting his eyes against the sun. Sure enough, there was no sign of his Harley.

Tack let the shade fall back into place. BJ's was on the other side of town, past the railroad tracks—at least a half hour on foot—while the ranch was only about a twenty-minute walk, fifteen if he took the shortcut he'd used after school as a kid.

He grinned, remembering the pathway that led directly past the creek and his favorite peach tree. Unwillingly, his gaze went to the soft indentation on the pillow next to him. The urge to turn and bury himself in the scent of her hit him hard and fast. He picked up the pillow and held it to his nose. Closing his eyes, he drank in the scent. *Peaches.* So sweet and warm and undeniably *her*.

He shook away the nostalgia and put the pillow down. It wasn't her. It never was when he opened his eyes. Never.

If only he knew the real woman's identity. Despite the regret swimming inside him, he also felt…different. More alive. Invigorated. She'd done that to him, with her body, her tears, her words.

Wait…it's been a long time. So long…

He searched for some memory, something distinctive, separate from his dream lover.

Nothing.

Cursing himself and that damn bottle of Cuervo, he headed for the bathroom. If he hurried, he could shower and change and make it to the ranch in time for his meeting with Gary Tucker, his father's attorney. Forever punctual, Gary was probably already at the ranch waiting, thrilled that Tack had agreed to come home for the reading of the will. No doubt he thought Tack was eager to get his hands on all that Brandon land and money.

But Tack hadn't wanted his father's legacy ten

years ago, and he sure as hell didn't want it now. He'd spent his entire youth indebted to a man who'd seen his only son as an extension of himself rather than an individual with his own likes and dislikes. As the only son and heir, Tack had been bound to the Brandon land, chained to a lifetime of tradition. He'd been this close to fulfilling his father's expectations, but only because of his mother. She'd loved the land as much as his father, but for different reasons. She'd never seen the ranch as a sign of wealth or power, but as her home.

She'd grown up on a neighboring spread, what was now the western portion of the Big B. An only child with a keen knowledge of cattle, she'd had dreams of taking over when her father passed on. The man, old and stubborn, refused to leave his single daughter—no matter how capable—in charge of thousands of acres of land. So she'd gone looking for a husband, and she'd found Cooper Brandon.

In his mother's eyes, Coop had been the perfect match. He'd been a rancher whose land bordered hers, one of the most eligible bachelors in the county, and most of all, her father had approved of him. Tack's mother had made a business proposition, and Cooper, greedy and eager to expand his cattle empire, had accepted.

Some say she'd been as cold as his father, but Tack didn't remember things that way. She'd always been kind and sweet, maybe a bit reserved, but some people didn't show their emotions as easily as others. Tack had forgiven her for that because whatever her shortcomings, at least she'd *tried* to be a good mother. But his father... There'd been no trying involved. Cooper Brandon had been a cattleman first, second and third, and his role as father had never figured in.

Tack's mother had died in a car accident the night of his senior prom and he'd left, determined to find his own way without the Brandon money and influence, without any help from his father, not that the man would have given any. Cooper Brandon would have sold his soul to keep his son on the Big B, but he wouldn't give the time of day to see him happy and content anywhere else.

Leaving had been hard. Making it even harder. But after years of blood, sweat and sacrifice, Tack had finally established a name for himself on the motocross and Supercross racing circuit. He'd raced for Team Suzuki, Yamaha, Honda and had just been approached to lead the Kawasaki team next year.

His gaze went to his duffel bag where he'd stuffed the new contracts that awaited his review and signature. He'd already received the go-ahead from his lawyer. A sweet deal, that's what Kenny had said. The best deal in the sport's history, and all because of Tack's reputation. One he'd built on his own.

No ties. No debts. *No roots.*

"Ain't nothing more important than this spread. The cattle, the land, it all comes first. Everything else is second."

The words echoed through Tack's mind, so crystal clear, as if his father had spoken them only yesterday.

Tack shook his head. He still couldn't believe

his father was dead. The man had thrived on life and all it had to offer—money, whiskey, and especially women—sometimes indulging too much, always demanding more than anyone had a right. So domineering and manipulative and...*alive*.

Even standing at the grave yesterday after everyone had left, Tack had felt somehow, someway there'd been a mistake. He'd half expected his father to walk up, slap him on the back and launch into one of his speeches about responsibility.

Dead.

There'd been no mistake, no escaping the present or the past, though Tack had tried. He'd headed for the nearest bar to get wrecked, to forget the last time he'd seen his father, the words they'd exchanged, the guilt that still ate at him. The hatred.

As if he could.

He would, he told himself as he pulled on a clean T-shirt and jeans, and dropped into the nearest chair to pull on his boots. Cooper Brandon was dead. Tack was sorry for that, but he couldn't bring the man back to life any more than he could go back and change their bitter parting over his mother's deathbed.

Tack could only face today, the future, and his involved a very important race in six weeks, the Northwestern 250cc championship, a title he had to win if he intended to lead the Kawasaki team.

If.

A loud knock seemed to rattle the walls and he winced. He yanked open the door just as a ring-adorned fist reared back, ready to pound some more and torture his temples.

"Well, I'll be," exclaimed the old woman standing on his doorstep. "It *is* you. Why, I saw you yesterday morning, smiling for them ESPN cameras and racing some fancy-schmancy bike of yours up near Palm Springs."

"That was a rerun, Effie. Palm Springs was six months ago."

"Six months?" Effie Coletrain, owner of the Inspiration Inn, frowned. "That damn TV's getting to be as bad as that tabloid trash everybody reads. You never know what's what."

Effie was in her late sixties, by Tack's estimation, but she made one hell of an attempt to hide it. Effie, alone, was responsible for the local Mary Kay rep's promotion from a pink Escort to the ultradeluxe pink Cadillac now zooming around town.

Today was no exception. Green eye shadow, hot-pink blush and matching lipstick worked to cover lines and wrinkles, but nothing could ease the rusty hint of her voice.

"Looks like somebody," she went on, "had himself a late night his first day back in town. Pastor Marley won't be too pleased about that. What other wicked things did you get yourself into last night?" Her gaze pushed past him.

He wedged his body between the open doorway and blocked her view. "Effie, I'm really in a hurry—"

"House rule number one—no carrying on in my establishment."

"Me?" He did his best to look innocent, the

way he had so many times in the past when he'd been as guilty as sin and Effie had demanded the truth.

She studied him with a narrowed gaze. "House rule number two—no lying to an old woman who's heard more than her share. I can see right into them lady-killer eyes of yours, Tack Brandon. And I definitely see a man who did some hunting last night." She peered past him. "What I don't see is anything left over from the kill."

"Rule number one for lady-killers," he said grinning. "Never leave evidence hanging around. You might incriminate yourself."

She stared him down a second more, then shook her head. "Same old smart mouth, I see." Her tone was stern, but her eyes were soft, indulgent, the way they'd been all those years ago when she'd shooed Tack and his two partners in crime, Jimmy and Jack Mission, into her office after they'd been caught pouring bubble bath into the motel's swimming pool.

She'd been mad as a bull, yet when the sheriff had shown up, she'd declined to file any charges. Instead, she'd handed all three boys brooms and put them to work sweeping the parking lot. Afterward, she'd given out homemade cookies and lemonade, and he'd liked her from then on.

He eyed the tray she carried. "That wouldn't be—"

"For breakfast?" She flashed him a what-kind-of-woman-do-you-think-I-am? look. "Don't you know all that sugar stunts your growth?"

"I'm all grown-up now."

"That's a matter of opinion," she snorted. "You

were too big for your britches when you were
waist-high, and you're still too big. I ought to put
you over my knee."

"You ought to, but you won't."

"Don't be so sure." She glared at him. "I'm not
as sweet as I used to be."

"You're still as sweet as ever," he said, trying to
coax a smile out of her. "Same old sweet-as-
molasses Effie."

She sighed and her expression softened. "You
got the old part right. Too old to be coming out
here waiting on the likes of you." She held up the
tray. "I don't usually offer room service—it's
breakfast bright and early at 7:00 a.m. sharp in my
dining room, or guests can fend for themselves,
but I made an exception, seeing as how you just
got back into town and all." She glanced at the
tray. "Home cookin' guaranteed to put a spring
in your step. And darlin', you sure as shootin'
look like you need it."

"I'll savor every bite," he promised.

"Good." Her brown eyes filled with sympathy.
"Your daddy was a bastard, but I always respected him. He was a straight-shooter. If he liked
you, he liked you. If he didn't, he didn't. You always knew where you stood with Coop. I'm real
sorry for you."

"Thanks, Effie." He took the tray from her
hands and slid it onto the nightstand.

"Eat up, son."

He was actually tempted as he shut the door
behind her and surveyed the meal she'd brought.
Other than the headache, he felt none of the usual
effects of a hangover. No churning stomach, ach-

ing muscles. Maybe he hadn't drunk as much as he'd thought.

Then why couldn't he remember more of last night? More of *her?*

The question niggled at him as he snatched his wallet off the dresser, grabbed a piece of sausage from the tray and headed out the door. Unfortunately, he didn't have time for a sit-down meal, not if he intended to make his meeting on time.

A soft whine stopped him just outside the motel room and he turned to see a pitiful-looking brown-and-white mutt—a cross between a German shepherd and a hound dog—eyeballing the sausage in his hands.

"Hey, buddy," he said, leaning down to stroke the animal's head. "You get lost on your way home?" Despite the question, Tack knew right away this was no one's pet.

The animal was painfully thin, his coat sticking to his ribs as if he hadn't eaten in weeks. The way the dog trembled beneath Tack's soothing hand made it obvious no one had petted him for a very, very long time.

"You hungry, Bones?"

Bones replied by gobbling up the sausage link and licking frantically at Tack's empty hand.

"There's more where that came from," he said as he unlocked the motel room and led the dog inside. He wondered briefly which one of Effie's rules sanctioned no stray dogs, not that he cared. He would pay Effie any fine she required. Tack had always had a soft spot for strays.

Leaving Bones near the doorway, he placed a blanket on the floor in the far corner. Next he filled the motel's ice bucket with water and placed it, along with the breakfast tray, near the blanket.

"It's all yours, Bones."

The dog hesitated only a few seconds before ambling forward to sniff the food. He licked his chops once, twice, then started gulping down the breakfast.

Tack stroked the dog's matted coat. "We'll clean you up later, then see about finding you a home. Right now, I'm afraid you're on your own, buddy. I've got business." The dog spared him a glance before turning back to his breakfast, and Tack knew he'd already been forgiven for leaving.

Just as Tack turned toward the doorway, his gaze snagged on a piece of white silk nestled between the tangled sheets. A pair of panties, he realized with a grin as he pulled the scrap of silk and lace free. He stared at the tiny pattern dotting the fabric, and the air caught in his chest. *Peaches.*

His fingers tightened as a detailed memory of last night washed over him. Her body pressed to his, her hands touching him just so, her voice whispering through his head, each syllable softened with a honey-sweet drawl... *Familiar.*

He shook his head and stuffed the undies into his pocket. It couldn't be. The last he knew of Annie Divine, she'd been dead set on leaving town, heading for college and a career, and a life *away* from her mother. Annie had hated her legacy even more than Tack had hated his.

It couldn't have been her.

IT WAS HER.

Tack stopped dead in his tracks and stared across the sea of wildflowers. He blinked once, twice, but she was still there. Dressed in a sheer white cotton sundress, angel hair spilling down around her shoulders like a silvery cloud, she could have been a vision, for all he knew. Or wishful thinking. She'd been on his mind since he'd started out from the motel.

But this was different. *She* was different. He'd pictured her the way she'd been ten years ago, a girl on the verge of womanhood, her figure just starting to blossom. No way had he anticipated the woman who stood before him. She was all grown-up now, her body fully developed, ripe with lush curves that inspired wicked thoughts.

Like mother, like daughter.

Wild Cherry Divine had been quite a looker in her day. It was no wonder his father had been hooked the moment she'd stepped into town, and out onto the stage at the Watering Trough, a strip joint out on Route 62. Cooper Brandon, married man, loving father and pillar of the community, had staked his claim early on, and Tack had despised him for it ever since.

Not that any of that had to do with Annie. She'd hated the connection between her mother and his father as much as he had, but they'd been kids, maybe eight or nine when the affair had started, and they'd had little say-so.

That was a long time ago.

For a full second, it struck him how much she'd changed, how much she resembled her mother. Then she lifted an expensive-looking camera hanging from a strap around her neck and started snapping pictures of a particular cluster of flowers.

He smiled. Annie and her camera. It was a sight he remembered well. Annie standing on the sidelines at a high school football game, snapping pictures of players, the crowd, the cheerleaders. Annie tagging along on a group picnic, lingering on the fringes of the crowd, taking shots of the picnic goers, the countryside, the local wildlife.

She'd been a photographer on the yearbook staff, attending every event, always trying to mesh with the "in" crowd. She never had. She'd always been Cherry Divine's daughter and that had set her apart, made her different, even though she'd done her best to fit in.

She fit perfectly here, he thought. She stood amid an ocean of daisies and bluebonnets. Her dress—sleeveless and short and sheer enough to make him swallow—revealed smooth, tanned arms and an endless pair of legs. The material molded to her full breasts and nipped at her small waist. A soft breeze ruffled her hair and teased her skirt even higher. She wasn't dressed to kill or painted with the latest cosmetics, yet she looked every bit as desirable as any model. She was real. Daughter of the earth. Mother Nature's finest work. If Eve had looked half as good, it was no wonder Adam had eaten that apple.

Tack bit into the peach he'd picked a few yards back near the creek, but he didn't taste the succulent fruit. He tasted her the way she'd been last night. Warm and sweet and so damn addicting...

A blast from the past.

A herd of horses couldn't have stopped him
from crossing the distance to her, from getting an
up-close-and-personal view of Miss Annie Divine. Maybe being back in Inspiration wouldn't
be as awful as he'd predicted. There was one
bright spot to this town. There always had been.
Annie.

3

"I NEVER KNEW you were a love-'em-and-leave-'em kind of girl." The deep voice startled Annie out of her inspection of a patch of bluebonnets. She whirled, fist flying through the air in a self-defense move her mother had taught her. Her hand connected with a rock-hard chest.

"Ouch!" A large, tanned hand rubbed the spot where she'd made contact. "Was I that bad last night?"

"Tack?" Her gaze swiveled up to see the man who'd crept up on her.

"In the flesh—ow!" He flinched as she punched him again. "I must've really stunk."

"That wasn't for last night. It was for sneaking up on me." She cradled her aching hand while her heart pounded at breakneck speed. "What are you doing out here?"

"The question, honey, is what are *you* doing out here?" he asked, biting into a half-eaten peach.

As his mouth worked at the sweet pulp, a trail of juice ran down his chin and she had the incredible urge to reach out, catch the drop and touch it to her own lips. Crazy. Touching him would be a mistake. Loving him last night had been an even worse mistake, but it was a sad truth she couldn't change. Better to forget and concentrate on today. Now. This moment.

Him.

Dark blue eyes caught and held hers, and she barely resisted the urge to turn and run. To avoid him and to avoid dealing with what had happened between them.

But Annie Divine didn't run. No matter how much she wanted to. She steeled her resolve and busied herself snapping a few pictures of a nearby cluster of daisies.

"You're a long way from Rose Street," he added.

"There isn't much to look at over there." Nothing but a big, run-down house and a neglected garden, neither of which she'd ever had the time to fix up. But that had changed. Cooper Brandon was dead now, Annie's debt was paid, her promise kept. Now she could get on with living.

She turned away from Tack and glanced at the surrounding landscape. "I come out here every once in a while. It's better when it's misty or foggy. Wildflowers photograph best in a subdued light, but early morning can lend itself to some good shots."

He motioned to her camera. "I figured you would have turned that into a career by now."

"I have. I'm a reporter for the *Inspiration In Touch*. I cover stories and do my own pictures."

"I wasn't talking about here. I thought maybe you'd gone big time. Houston, Dallas, maybe even out of state."

"Plans change. My mama got sick right after you left and so I stayed to take care of her."

"I heard she died. I'm sorry."

She met his gaze. "You never liked her."

"True enough, but I'm still sorry. Sorry for you."

"And I'm sorry for you. You missed a beautiful funeral yesterday."

He shrugged, his expression closing, and she knew she'd touched a subject better left alone. "So you like this place, huh?" he went on, as if eager to move to a safer topic.

She cast a sweeping glance around her and a sad smile curved her lips. "It holds a certain charm."

Blue eyes twinkled in the sunlight. "Last time I looked, you weren't too fond of Brandon land."

"It's been a long time since you looked."

He stared at her for a drawn-out moment. Insects buzzed, birds chirped and her heart double-thumped. A gleam lit his eyes. "I'd say too long, judging by last night." He pitched what was left of the fruit and rubbed his hands together. "You hightailed it out pretty early this morning. I didn't even have a chance to say hello."

"I'm not much for conversation." She did her best to ignore the whirlwind rushing through her. The regret. The elation. The despair. The joy. It was a volatile mix, one that threatened to send tears streaming down her face.

But not in front of Tack. That's where her mother had made her mistake. She'd let Cooper Brandon see what she felt for him. By pouring out her love, she'd fortified the hold he already had over her. Annie refused to do the same, to wear her emotions on her sleeve. It was better to keep them buried, to stay in control.

Not that she *loved* him. Not now. Not ever again.

"We could have skipped the pillow talk then," he went on. "And said hello another way." He reached out, his fingertip skimming her cheek. Electricity sizzled along her nerve endings.

Eager for a distraction, she turned away and studied the landscape as if she were searching for just the right amount of light and shadow to add texture to her next photograph. "I had to get home and I didn't see any point in waking you. You really tied one on last night. I'm..." She swallowed. "I'm surprised you even remembered what we...what happened."

"I remember, all right." His voice, so deep and smooth, slid into her ears and made her insides quiver. "You and me, together. What I don't remember is how we ended up—" his hand closed over her shoulder and forced her to face him "—*together*."

"You were drunk and Bobby Jack thought it was better if you didn't drive home. He asked me to give you a ride."

A slow, wicked smile spread across his face.

"Not that kind of a ride. A lift back to your motel."

His smile widened. "Then the ride."

She frowned. "Haven't your hormones calmed down since the twelfth grade?"

"I thought so," he said seriously, "until last night." He grinned and gave her a wink. "But then, you always did get me hot and bothered, honey."

His words stirred so many old memories. Quick kisses beneath the bleachers after a Friday-night football game. Endless necking sessions in the bed of his daddy's pickup. Midnight swims down by the lake.

Despite her determination to stay cool and aloof and unaffected, a smile tugged at her lips. "You were forever trying to get into my pants."

"And last night you seduced me right out of mine."

"*I* seduced *you?*"

"You undressed me. I don't remember much, but I distinctly remember looking down and see-ing you unzip my pants. *Feeling* you unzip them."

"The material was soaking-wet and the air con-ditioner was stuck. If I'd have left you in those damp things, you would have come down with pneumonia." She reached into the camera bag at her feet and pulled out a zoom-lens attachment. *Stay busy,* she told herself. *Then you won't have to look at him.* "And don't call me honey."

"A convenient excuse, and I like calling you honey." Before she could stop him, he slipped one strong arm around her waist and pulled her close. The lens attachment sailed to the soft grass and the camera sagged against its strap. Tack leaned down, his lips skimming the side of her neck as he took a whiff. "Because you smell so sweet."

She managed to get one hand between them and push him away, a halfhearted gesture that did little to ease the thunder of her heart. "I'd appreciate it if you didn't ruin my camera equipment."

He glanced at the piece lying in the grass. "If it's broken, I'll buy you a new one."

"That's not the point."

"Then what is the point?"

"That you've got your arm around me when I don't want it around me."

He pulled her closer and the camera jabbed into her stomach, just an inch above the spot where a very prominent part of his anatomy was doing some jabbing of its own.

"I didn't see you putting up a fuss last night."

"That was then." She tried to keep her voice from sounding as breathless as she suddenly felt. "This is now."

His eyes glittered. "Not up to ripping my clothes off and taking advantage of me again?"

"You can think what you want about last night, but I did have noble intentions. At first, anyway." She shook her head and stared at a point just over his shoulder, anywhere to keep from looking into his eyes, from losing herself in them the way she'd lost herself less than ten hours ago. After all these years, he still set the butterflies loose in her stomach. She stiffened and fought back the feeling. "Could you please let me go?"

Catching her chin, he urged her to meet his gaze. He stared at her long and hard, as if trying to see inside. "You know, I could always tell what you were thinking, Annie. Always. Everything was always right there in your eyes, on your face."

"And now?"

"It's different." He released her with a puzzled shake of his head. "You're different."

"Ten years is a long time." She turned away from him. "People change." She snatched up the zoom attachment, walked a few feet away and tried to concentrate on attaching the new lens to her camera. "If you don't mind, I came out here for some quiet time." *Go away, go away, go away,* she silently begged.

"We need to talk." He came up behind her.

She inched forward. "About what?"

"About last night."

"What about it?"

"We slept together."

"And?"

"And—" he sounded exasperated "—we *slept* together."

She aimed her camera and zoomed in on a vibrant-looking daisy. "And?"

"Dammit, Annie." His hand closed over her upper arm and pulled her back around to face him. "There are things we need to talk about."

"Like what?"

"Like what's bothering you."

She had to hand it to him. He looked genuinely concerned. For the space of a heartbeat, she wanted to throw her arms around him and tell him how mixed-up she felt. That she was glad he was home, and sad at the same time. That last night had been wonderful, yet heartbreaking. That she wanted him to stay almost as much as she wanted him to leave.

"Nothing's bothering me," she managed to say in her most nonchalant voice.

"Then how do you feel?"

"Fine. I was sneezing a few days ago, but the reason for it turned out to be a high pollen count in the air."

"That's not what I'm talking about." He ran a frustrated hand through his hair. "How do you feel about what we...*did* last night?"

"We had sex."

"Jesus, Annie." He threw up his hands. "I think it was a little more than that. This is you and me we're talking about. We have a history. We were friends. I was your first."

"Okay, it was great sex. Nostalgic sex. Making-up-for-lost-time sex. It was still just sex."

"*Sex?*" He gave her an incredulous look.

"As in two people satisfying mutual urges. I was needy, you were needy, we happened to be needy at the same time."

"That's really all it was to you?"

"Why are you making a big deal out of this?"

"Because it *is* a big deal."

"Why?"

"Because..." He seemed to grapple for words. "Because there...there are consequences."

"Like what?"

"Like..." He gave her a stern look. "Like you could be pregnant for one."

"I'm on the Pill." Instead of looking relieved, he simply stared at her as if she'd just grown an eye in the middle of her forehead. "Geez, Tack, don't look so shocked. A lot of women take birth control pills."

"We're not talking about a lot of women, we're talking about you. *You*, the girl who nearly had a fit when I suggested it that time before we…got together. No way, you said. You were convinced everybody would think you were loose like—"

"My mother," she finished for him. "That was then," she repeated, "and this is now. I'm not an ignorant teenager anymore. I'm twenty-eight years old." And irregular, she added silently. And that was the only reason she'd gone on the Pill even though her best friend and editor, Deb, had hooted and hollered that now was the time for Annie to start having some fun. "And I take responsibility for myself. There's no need for you to worry about any little surprises popping out in nine months." She pulled the camera from around her neck and packed it away in her bag. "I really need to get going."

"We're not finished." His fingers closed around her wrist.

She pulled her hand free, zipped up her camera bag and glared at him. "You're making an awful big deal about this. There's no chance I'm pregnant, so what's the problem?" Understanding dawned a heartbeat later and her mouth dropped open. "You're not trying to tell me… Oh, no! I can't believe I'm so stupid. Stupid, stupid, *stupid*."

"What are you talking about?"

She turned an accusing stare on him. "You have some sort of communicable disease, don't you? That's what this interrogation is all about. You're trying to find a way to tell me you contracted some deadly disease and now my insides are going to shrivel up and fall out and—"

"Hold on a second. For the record, I just had

my yearly physical last week, including a blood test, and I'm as healthy as a racehorse." At her obvious skepticism, he added, "Despite my enthusiasm last night, I'm not in the habit of picking up women. And whenever I am with a woman, I use a condom. And I have a clean bill of health from the best damn team doctor in L.A. to prove it."

"Well—" she took a deep breath and tried to calm her panicked nerves "—that's a relief."

"Not completely." He folded his arms. "Since we're cleaning out closets, is there anything I should know about? I don't want anything shriveling up and falling off either."

"Because of me?" She bristled. "I certainly don't have any sort of disease."

"And what about your past partners?"

Past partners? As if she had any. She shook her head. "Nothing to worry about there."

He didn't seem convinced. "How many have you had?"

"Why does it matter?"

"Because I don't like playing Russian roulette."

"You weren't very concerned last night."

"I was barely conscious last night—" His words died as his gaze dropped to her hand. Relief smoothed his suddenly tense expression. "At least you're not married."

She erupted then. "Of course I'm not married! Geez, do you think I would have slept with you if I were?" She poked a finger at his chest. "What kind of person do you think I am?"

Like your mother. He didn't have to say the words. She knew what he was thinking, what everyone was always thinking. The trouble was, it didn't hurt with everyone else. She'd stopped caring about what the people of Inspiration thought a long time ago, with the exception of the few she called friends. But Tack...

"Look, Annie, I didn't mean—" The honk of a horn drowned out the rest of his words. Both Annie and Tack turned just as a Jeep topped the horizon and plowed across the pasture headed straight for them.

"I'd just about given up on you, boy." Gary Tucker shouted to Tack as he brought the vehicle to a jarring halt and killed the engine. Clad in jeans, a chambray work shirt and faded cowboy boots, the man looked more like a ranch hand than an attorney. "Would have, but then one of the boys said he passed by the road over yonder and saw you out here talking to Annie. Come on." He lifted his cowboy hat to brush back his gray hair. "I'll give you two a lift."

"What do you say, honey? Can we drop you someplace?"

"Actually—" she met his stare "—I was headed your way."

Tack's forehead wrinkled in a frown. "The house? Why?"

"For the reading of the will," Gary interjected. "Coop left specific instructions that he wanted Annie there."

Tack's attention shifted from Gary to Annie, and his blue eyes narrowed. "Why would my father want you at the reading of his will? Last I knew, you didn't like him, he didn't like you."

She shrugged, despite the sudden pounding of

her heart. "We got to know each other these past few years."

"You and my father?"

"Turned out to be pretty good friends," Gary said, climbing from the seat of the Jeep.

"You and my father?" Tack repeated, as if the words wouldn't register in his brain. "But you always hated him."

"Half the county did." Gary slid a protective arm around Annie's shoulder. "But Annie changed that, didn't you, gal? Softened that old hellion right up."

"*You* and my *father?*" he said, the words more accusation than question as anger chased shock across his handsome features.

She summoned her courage and met his murderous glare. "I never actually hated him, Tack. I never really knew him. Once I took the time, I realized he was a good man."

"I'll just bet he was good." Blue eyes drilled into hers and she came this close to taking a step back. "What I want to know, honey, is just how good he was. And more importantly, was he better than last night?"

4

ANNIE FIXED her gaze on the sprawling ranch house just up ahead and tried to ignore the man seated directly behind her.

Was he better than last night? Her face still burned from the question. Not because he'd asked right in front of Gary. The attorney was too much of a gentleman to even acknowledge the question. He'd simply started toward the Jeep as if Tack hadn't said anything out of the ordinary. She wasn't embarrassed. No, she was mad at herself for not telling Tack right away that she was doing more out this way than simply taking pictures.

She chanced a peek in the side mirror and saw him staring back at her. *Traitor*, his gaze seemed to say, and she couldn't blame him. He was right. While she'd never slept with Cooper Brandon, she had befriended him. She'd given up her anger and her principles to embrace a man she'd never held anything but contempt for, and she'd done it willingly.

Look out for him, Annie. Don't let him hurt alone. It had been her mother's dying plea, and Annie's last promise.

She'd approached Cooper after her mother's funeral, to set aside her resentment and offer thanks that he'd come, that he'd sent vanload after vanload of fresh daisies—her mother's favorite. It had been little more than an automatic response, a proper display of politeness. But it had turned on her. She'd touched his arm and he'd faced her, his usually hard eyes shining with remorse, guilt, affection. At that moment, Annie had actually softened toward Cooper. Over the next few years, she'd even started to understand him.

She felt Tack's gaze in the mirror, but she refused to look. It didn't matter what he thought of her. She didn't owe him the time of day, much less an ounce of loyalty, an explanation or an apology. She'd befriended his father and too bad if he didn't approve. She didn't have to justify herself to him.

Despite what they'd shared ten years ago.

And last night.

It shouldn't have happened. No matter how right it had felt, how wonderful. They were too different. Just as his father and her mother had been worlds apart, wrong for each other because of where they came from and where they were going, so were Annie and Tack.

Annie was Wild Cherry Divine's daughter. Tack would never forgive her for that. Or more importantly, for the fact that she no longer wanted his forgiveness. She was who she was. No longer ashamed. Or regretful. And she wasn't falling in love with him again.

Unfortunately, she was all too aware of his proximity. With each passing moment, her breaths grew shallow. Her heartbeat stampeded like a team of frightened horses, particularly when the Jeep hit a nasty rut in the road. The truck lurched and Tack's hand closed over the edge of the seat just a fraction shy of touching Annie's shoulder.

"...the house hasn't changed much."

Gary's voice pushed past the pounding in her ears and she focused on the words, intent on gathering her control and ignoring Tack. Mind over matter, she told herself. *Your mind over his matter.*

"Coop did have the foreman's house remodeled for Eli and his wife," Gary went on.

"Eli's *married*?" Tack shook his head in disbelief. "The same Eli who's been cowboying for my father since he was fifteen? The same Eli who used to brand those little x's into the side of the bunkhouse for every woman he talked into bed?"

Gary chuckled. "Kept track for more than twenty years. A few more brands and the wall would have dissolved in a heap of ashes."

"I never figured him for the marrying kind."

"Got himself a couple of kids, too. Twin boys, 'round seven or eight, and a baby on the way. Wife's name is Vera."

"Vera Marley? The preacher's daughter? But she hated Eli."

"That's what everybody thought," Annie said, praying she didn't sound as breathless as she felt. But she needed to talk, to do something besides feel the way Tack's deep voice, his presence, affected her. "I think Vera and Eli were more shocked than anybody. One minute they were fighting. The next thing you know, Eli kisses Vera, she kisses him, and the war was over."

"That was on Friday," Gary added. "Went on their first date Saturday night, got engaged Sunday, much to her daddy's upset, married at the judge's office on Monday and been together nine years now."

"Nine years. Talk about luck." Tack's voice sent a waterfall of heat cascading down Annie's spine. Her nipples tingled, her thighs burned, and she remembered his words the night before. *Best luck I've had in a hell of a long time.*

"Not luck," Annie replied before she could stop herself. "Love. There's a big difference."

"HE DID *WHAT*?" The question echoed off the walls of Cooper Brandon's study. Tack bolted from a brown leather chair to tower over his father's desk, where Gary sat reading the man's last will and testament.

The attorney slipped off his glasses and met Tack's stare. "He left that stretch of wildflowers that borders the south road to Annie. An acre and a half, to be exact. The rest, as you've been told, goes to you."

"I don't believe it." Tack tried to digest the news while Annie barely resisted the urge to jump from her seat and shout for joy. Coop had given her more than an acre of land, or more importantly, *the* acre and a half of land.

"He gave away Brandon land? My father handed over some of his precious ranch? That's crazy. He would never let any of it fall into outside hands. When Clem and his wife moved into that old deserted cabin down by the river after their place burned, he called the sheriff and had them thrown off. *Thrown off*, for Christ's sake. They didn't have anyplace to go, not a penny to their name, but he didn't care. They weren't Brandons, and this is Brandon land, he said. He wouldn't give one square inch away." His gaze strayed to the portrait of Cooper Brandon, looking so serious and stiff, on the far wall. Tack just stared, long and hard, the muscles in one jaw working as if he wanted to rip the thing from its mount. "He couldn't have been in his right mind."

Annie didn't miss the strange light in his eyes, the turmoil, and she barely resisted the urge to reach out. Instead, she curled her fingers into the rich leather of the armchair where she sat.

"He was lucid, all right," the attorney went on. "Sane right up until he shut his eyes for good, and this was one thing he insisted on. He wanted to make things right."

"My point exactly," Tack said angrily. "Cooper Brandon didn't go around doing the right thing. He did what was most lucrative for this ranch, and giving away land isn't very lucrative." He turned to Annie. "Why?"

Her gaze met his. "Because that land means something to me."

"Why?" he persisted. He smiled, but there was nothing friendly about his eyes. Something dangerous, maybe. Very dangerous. "You and my old man have fond memories of the place?"

"Something like that."

Tack's expression drew tight as images filled

his mind. Annie talking with his father, laughing and smiling and...

Anger rushed through him like flame eating up a fuse.

"The two of you have romantic picnics out there?" he pressed. "Go stargazing? Have a little roll in the wildflowers?" He saw a glimmer of pain in her eyes, then it vanished and there was no indication his words had affected her.

She didn't show a damn thing, but he knew she hurt, because he hurt. Saying it, thinking it, feeling it. Christ! Annie and his *fath—*

A pounding on the front door echoed through the house and shattered the dangerous thought.

"Tack Brandon!" came Effie Coletrain's muffled shout from outside, followed by several frantic barks. "You get on out here and get this mangy mutt that ripped apart my motel room!"

"I really need to get going." Annie stuffed the deed Gary handed her into her camera bag. "Thanks for everything, Gary."

"Tell me, Annie." Tack's voice followed her to the door. He needed to hear the truth from her, to wipe away the niggling doubts, the confusion. "What could mean so much that Coop Brandon would give up a piece of his precious land? *What?*"

"My mother," came her calm, cool voice as she paused in the doorway. "She's buried there."

"IT'S SATURDAY." Deb Strickland, the editor of the town's only newspaper, stood across the room, coffeepot in one hand, ceramic mug in the other, and gave Annie an accusing stare. "What are you doing here?"

"I usually work Saturdays." Annie set her camera bag on her desk and turned on her computer.

"I know, but the funeral was yesterday." Deb finished pouring and headed for Annie.

Dressed in a red silk blouse, matching skirt and three-inch stiletto heels, the brunette looked as if she should be walking a runway rather than cracked linoleum. She sipped steaming black coffee from a mug that read 100% Bitch and eyed Annie. "I thought you might want the day off."

"I haven't taken a day off in over three years."

"My point exactly. You're due."

"I'm all right, Deb." Or she would be once she settled down at her desk and put the morning behind her. *Distance.*

"I know I probably seemed like a real witch because I didn't go to the funeral, but ever since my granny died, anything involving cemeteries really creeps me out. Just because I wasn't there for you yesterday, though, doesn't mean I'm not here for you now. Take the day off or cry on my shoulder, or whatever you feel like doing."

"Coop and I were friends and I'll miss him, but he's gone. I just want to have a normal day. Business as usual, okay?"

"Are you sure?" Deb gave her a searching glance. At Annie's nod, she finally shrugged. "If that's what you want." The expression of sympathy on her face faded into her typical I'm-the-boss look as she glanced at her watch. "You're an hour late." She took another sip of coffee and headed for her desk.

Deb slid into the role of slave driver so easily, but it was more for show than anything else. The *Inspiration In Touch* was a typical small-town newspaper with only Deb, Annie and Wally Wilkins, a nineteen-year-old journalism major, on the payroll. The three of them were like family. They put out a weekly edition with a Friday deadline and a Sunday distribution. Deb took care of the advertising, edited and did a few columns, while Annie covered the news and took all the pictures, and Wally did his best to convince both women that he should be doing more than running copy or fixing the ancient printing press that was forever breaking down. They bickered, laughed and supported one another.

Deb and Wally were the only two things about Inspiration Annie knew she'd miss.

She opened her planner, as she did every Saturday morning, to go over her weekly schedule and get ready for a new edition. *Business as usual.*

She told herself that, but the tremble in her thighs, the ache between her legs, refused to be ignored.

Had she really slept with Tack?

Yes, and the trouble was, she wanted to do it again.

Not that she would. She might have been weak last night, seeing him in the flesh after all these years. She'd been in love with him, after all. Precisely the reason she wouldn't sleep with him again.

Annie wasn't going to risk falling in love all over again. Not the I'll-love-you-'til-my-dying-breath kind of love her mother had had for Cooper Brandon. Annie had watched the woman throw away so many hopes and dreams for a man, and she wasn't going to make the same mistake.

With Tack Brandon it would be all too easy. Ten years hadn't dulled his looks or his charm or the way he made her feel when he smiled. Warm and hungry and oblivious to everything except him.

That was the *real* trouble.

"Annie?" Deb's voice penetrated her thoughts. "You're not all right, are you? I'm sorry. I shouldn't have said anything about you being late, but I was just going through the motions—"

"It's not you."

"—because you know I completely understand your being late, I just thought you wanted me to act like my bitchy self—"

"It's not you. It's me."

"I knew it. You're upset about Coop."

"No. I'm just tired, that's all." Tired? Since when did she make excuses to Deb? Not only her editor, but her best friend? She didn't. Not anymore. Not since she'd promised herself never to let other people's opinions of her dictate who she was. Annie Divine had taken control of her own life, and she intended to keep it. "I had a late night because—" Her words faded into the shrill ring of the newspaper's hotline, a bright red phone that occupied the corner of Deb's desk.

"Hold that thought." Deb snatched up the line. "*Inspiration In Touch*, you're in touch with Deb." Seconds later, Deb slid the receiver into place, a knowing grin on her face. "You're tired because you picked up a cowboy."

"Says who?"

"Effie Coletrain just informed me that Tack Brandon, *the* Tack Brandon, Supercross superstar and the long lost son of Cooper Brandon, rolled back into town yesterday. Good sources have it that he rolled straight to BJ's, got rip-roaring drunk and you gave him a lift back to his motel *and* went inside. And didn't leave until much, much later." At Annie's incredulous stare, Deb shrugged. "Hazards of living in a small town. Gossip spreads like wildfire." A gleam lit her eyes and she clapped her hands. "I don't believe it. Goody-goody Annie finally got down and dirty with a lean, mean, cow-punching machine!"

She fought back the sudden pounding of her heart and gathered her composure. "I am not a goody-goody."

"Trust me, you're about as goody-goody as they get—I don't care what folks used to say about your mama." Deb perched on the edge of Annie's desk, took a sip of coffee and beamed. "I thought you looked different this morning. Your cheeks are flushed."

"That's because my air conditioner went out last night and I spent the morning in hell." Then, of course, she'd met up with the devil when she'd been taking a few early-morning pictures.

"Effie said you two were an item once."

"Effie talks too much."

"So she lied?"

Annie shrugged. "We went out a few times."

"As in, let's do homework together or let's get naked in the back seat?"

"As in, I had a crush on him throughout high school and he rarely glanced my way. One night, after our senior homecoming game, he offered to give me a lift home. He was always doing things like that, always helping people. He used to carry Pattie Mitchell's tuba every day. Fatty Pattie— that's what the boys called her—was so shy. She never smiled, but Tack always took the time to coax one out of her and tote that tuba to the Band Hall. He used to help old Mrs. Witherspoon down the aisle at church, too. She had a walker and a hip replacement. The other kids would make fun of her, but not Tack." He'd been so determined to accept people for who they were, to see beyond looks, wealth, power, the way his father never had. To be different from the bastard Coop had been back then."

"Sounds like a saint."

"Sometimes." And at other times, he'd been every bit the sinner, with his wicked grins and his sweet, intoxicating kisses.

"Annie?"

"Um, yeah?"

"You were saying?"

Annie forced the image of Tack away and cleared her throat. "I, um, thought he was just being nice."

"But he secretly lusted after you?"

"Not at first. But once we talked and got to know each other—"

"Then he lusted after you."

"Sort of." At Deb's get-real look, Annie added, "Okay, so he lusted after me."

"And you lusted after him."

"Yes," Annie admitted. "We went out several times and became a couple until our senior prom. His mother had a car accident late that night. We spent half the night pacing the emergency room, waiting for the doctors to do what they could, and waiting for Tack's father to show up."

"Where was he?"

"With my mother. He didn't get word and make it to the hospital until ten minutes after they'd pronounced Tack's mother dead. He and Coop got into a fight and he left." Annie shook her head. She could still smell the disinfectant, feel the cold floor seeping up through the soles of her shoes as she'd sat there and watched him storm away without so much as a backward glance. Her heart had hurt so bad. Not for herself, for her own loss, but for his.

That's the way it had always been with Tack. She found herself so caught up in the sight and sound and feel of him that her own needs fell by the wayside.

"He left you? Just like that?"

"We weren't exactly married." While Annie knew he'd cared for her, she'd never had any illusions about Tack Brandon loving her the way she'd loved him. When he left, she'd hurt, but she'd also understood, and later, she'd been grateful for the hard lesson learned. "We were kids. He did what he had to do under the circumstances. End of story."

Deb gave her a searching glance. "Sounds like you guys started working on a sequel last night."

Annie averted her gaze and searched through her drawer for a computer disk. "Last night was just overactive hormones. It was bound to happen. You said so yourself, if I kept going home alone, my hormones were going to erupt one day and I'd find myself grabbing a little gusto with the first cowboy I could find. Well, I went into hormone overload and Tack just happened to be there."

"You're not still carrying a torch for this guy, are you?"

"Of course not." She retrieved the disk and turned to rearranging some of her notes. "Why is everybody making such a big deal out of this? It was only sex. It's the nineties. I'm a healthy woman. I'm entitled to a little fun."

"*Fun* being the operative word. You should be smiling right now, honey—" Her words faded into another shrill ring of the hotline.

A few seconds later, Deb turned to Annie.

"Don't tell me. Another update on my sex life."

"No, though I'd be glad to hear it because I think you're holding back. It was Tess Johnson. Shotzi just had her litter."

"Shotzi?"

"Tess's prizewinning pig, the one that took first place at the FFA championships in Dallas last spring. She just had the largest recorded litter in Texas in fifty years. I'd do this one myself, but I've got an interview for the This Is Your Neighbor column, then a manicure at the beauty salon."

A pig? "Remind me again why you left the *Dallas Star?*"

"Because my father owns the *Star*, and everybody who works for him." Deb grabbed her briefcase and purse. "That's why I took the money my granny left me when she passed on and reinvested it in this place. It's small, but it's mine, and it does have its advantages. You don't have to go neck and neck with some ruthless colleagues to get the best stories."

"You're right. I'd hate to have to worry about someone stealing the Johnson-pig exclusive right out from under me. Why don't you send Wally?"

"He's not ready."

"Who's not ready?" Wally, his shoulder-length blond hair pulled back in a ponytail, spectacles perched low on his nose, crested the back staircase and walked into the office. Black newsprint covered his hands and forearms. "I've got two years at the local community college and I'm ready for anything."

"In time, grasshopper." Deb did her best *Kung Fu* imitation, and Wally frowned.

"Discrimination." He leaned down and started rummaging in a cabinet. "That's what this is. Give the guy all the manual labor, make him fight with a dadblastit press that keeps spraying ink everywhere." He paused to pull out a bottle of cleaning solution. "And save the good stuff for yourselves."

"Good stuff?" Annie shook her head. "As in pigs? Yeah, right, Wally."

"Come on, Annie," Deb said. "I bet they're cute."

"I'm sure they are, but after covering that baby raccoon stuck up in Mr. Miller's tree last year, I promised myself no more animal exclusives."

"That was a great story."

"The raccoon attacked me."

"He was just a little scared of the flash."

"He went berserk. I had to have a rabies shot at the hospital over in Georgetown."

"She gets to have all the fun," Wally grumbled as he yanked open another cabinet and launched into a search for extra rags.

"How long do those rabies things last?" Deb asked.

"A few years."

"So you're all set in case the pigs decide to gang up on you." Deb gulped the last of her coffee. "Gotta go or I'll be late for my interview." She paused in the doorway. "So is Tack Brandon really as cute as Effie Coletrain said?"

Annie stuffed a notebook into her purse. "How many pigs did you say Shotzi had?"

"Come on, Annie. I'm not from around here, remember? Give me a hint. Blond or brunette?"

"And it's the biggest recorded litter, you say?"

"The biggest?" Wally slammed the cabinet shut. "Aw, man, she gets all the breaks." He stomped back down the stairs.

"Bulky or lean in the muscle department?" Deb smiled and resumed her line of questioning.

Annie grabbed two extra rolls of film from her top desk drawer and stuffed them in her case. "I'll check with the *Farmer's Almanac* and the state FFA group just to get my facts straight. They keep track of all those things."

"You know, Annie, it's all right to let your hair down once in a while, despite what all those old biddies down at the bingo hall might say. You should call up your cowboy and go for round two. Use it before you lose it, honey," Deb said before she closed the door behind her.

If only it were that simple.

But Tack Brandon wasn't just some cowboy Annie had picked up to satisfy her needs as she'd said. He was *the* cowboy. With bedroom eyes and a heart-thumping smile that made her think beyond long nights filled with mind-blowing sex. To weddings and babies and happily-ever-afters.

A man she could fall in love with all over again if she gave herself the chance.

Which she wasn't about to do.

She had a future that didn't include him. She longed for front-page stories and bigger bylines, and now that her promise to her mother had been fulfilled, she could make her dreams come true. She would. Yesterday, after she'd said goodbye to Coop, she'd stopped at the post office and mailed off résumés and tear sheets—page samples of her work—to the editors of the top five newspapers on her Top Twenty list, with Deb's full support. Meanwhile, Annie would seize every opportunity to beef up her portfolio.

Or in this case, pork it up.

Grabbing her camera equipment and purse, she headed downstairs. Today was the first day of the rest of Annie Divine's life, and she intended to make the most of it.

5

"MY LIFE STINKS." Annie stared down at her soiled dress later that afternoon and grimaced.

"I've got news for you, girlfriend. It isn't your life. It's you." Annie glared and Deb smiled. "Fieldwork is tough. Think of this as training."

That's exactly what she'd been thinking as she'd fled *sixteen* squealing piglets, only half the litter, and run straight into a mud puddle. She sniffed. At least she'd thought it was mud.

"You should have sent me." Wally sat at a nearby desk compiling ads for next week's edition. "I raised two pigs in high school and I know what makes them oink. But does anybody listen? Heck, no."

Deb ignored Wally and turned back to Annie. "I guess you're not up for drinks at BJ's."

Annie leaned down to tug off her mud-covered sandals. "The only thing I'm up for is a nice, long soak in a hot bath."

"Now that sounds like the best idea I've heard all day." The deep voice rumbled up and down Annie's spine and she froze in place.

Then her head snapped up and she found herself staring at jean-covered hips. She straightened, and her attention shifted slowly upward to drink in the man who stood in the doorway. Her gaze roamed over a trim waist, a crisp white T-shirt stretched over a broad chest, to a stubbled jaw, before colliding with twinkling blue eyes, as blue as a rain-washed sky. The air snagged in her chest.

"You must be Tack Brandon," Deb said.

"Tack?" Wally pushed his glasses up to take a good look. "Well, bust my behind, you *are* him! *The* Tack Brandon. The motocross racer."

Tack winked and stopped in front of Annie's desk. "The last time I looked."

"What are you doing here?" Annie blurted, all too aware of Deb's smile and Wally's curious expression.

"You forgot something." He pulled a white pair of panties dotted with tiny peaches from his pocket.

Annie's heart stopped beating, Wally chuckled and Deb barely caught a giggle as Tack dangled the skimpy silk from one tanned finger.

"I, um, we really have to get going." Deb motioned for Wally. "I'm dead tired and it's way past Wally's bedtime." Before Annie could blink, Deb hauled Wally from his desk and they both disappeared into the darkened stairwell.

"I thought you might need these." Tack rubbed the silky material between his two fingers in a sensuous caress she felt from her head, clear to the tips of her toes, even though he wasn't touching her.

Ah, but he had. That was the trouble. That had always been the trouble. One touch made her want another. And another.

Heat uncoiled in her stomach, along with a

slow burning anger that spread through her. She came so close to snatching the panties from his hand, but she wasn't about to give him the satisfaction of knowing she was the least bit affected by him.

Calm, cool, indifferent. The silent mantra echoed in her head and she shrugged. "Thanks for the gesture, but I'm wearing new ones."

"Then I'll just keep these." He stuffed them into his shirt pocket and perched on the corner of her desk. "So this is where you work?"

"It isn't the *Times*, but a girl has to start somewhere." Her gaze narrowed. "Is that why you came? To see where I work?"

"Actually—" his voice took on a softer note and she read the regret in his eyes "—I wanted to say I'm sorry about today, about the things I said. Gary told me you and Coop were just friends, and I had no call to act like such a jerk—"

"A slime bucket," she cut in.

"A creep," he conceded.

"A bast—"

"Ouch, Annie," he interjected. "You sure know how to hurt a guy." His grin dissolved into a serious expression. "But I know I deserve it. I was way out of line. It's just the thought of you and him and... It made me a little crazy."

"I didn't sleep with him, but I was still his friend. No more, but no less."

"Because your mother asked you to," he pointed out.

"And that makes a difference?"

"It shouldn't, should it?" He raked tense fingers through his dark hair. "But it does. I'm not thrilled with the idea of you and him being friends—I can't quite understand it—but I'm not mad. I'm just sorry for drilling you about the land the way I did." His sensuous lips curved in a teasing grin. "Sorry for being a jerk/slime bucket/creep/bastard."

"Apology accepted." A smile tugged at her lips despite her best efforts to remain aloof.

Indifferent.

"So you forgive me?"

She eyed him a long moment and saw the sincerity in the blue depths of his gaze. "Maybe."

"I was hoping for a yes."

"It's the closest you're going to get."

"I'll take it." He winked. "And since you're being so charitable, how about doing a job for me? I need somebody to take pictures of the ranch so prospective buyers can see what they're getting."

Buyers. As in…

"You're *selling?*" He nodded and Annie's stomach went hollow. "But that ranch has been in your family for years," she pointed out. "Your father lived and breathed that place. Your mother, too. It's part of them. They're a part of it."

"But I'm not." He shook his head. "Hell, Annie, I never was. I pretended for a long time, but it's just not in my blood. I know my mother would want it to stay in the hands of a rancher who would love it the way she did. I can't. I never could."

"When?" she asked, tamping down the strange ache the notion stirred. Selling was good. *Great.* No Tack, no temptation, no falling in love.

"A month or so to circulate a sales package and

find a prospective buyer, a cattleman—the Big B is a ranch and it'll stay that way. Every hand stays on as part of the sale, for the next year anyway. I want the cowboys to have a chance to prove themselves to a new boss."

A strange sense of admiration crept through her. For all his bitterness, Tack had grown into a fair and decent man. Just like the fair and decent boy who'd helped old Mrs. Witherspoon down the aisle in church every Sunday.

She forced the feeling aside and asked, "In the meantime?"

"I'll be staying at the ranch until it's sold. Eli isn't used to running things on his own."

"What about your racing?"

"I'm not due in L.A. for another six weeks. I'll bring in some bikes, do laps out in one of the unused pastures in the morning and oversee the ranch during the day."

"Sounds like you have everything figured out."

"Almost everything." His blue gaze pinned her to her chair. "So much has changed." *You*, his eyes seemed to say.

She shrugged. "You can't expect time to stand still, even in Inspiration. We've got cable television, and Mabel at the beauty shop had a tanning bed installed, and Mitch Freeman's running a computer-repair shop out of the back of his feed store."

"That's not what I was talking about."

"Effie Coletrain even put in a whirlpool spa over at the motel," she went on as if she hadn't heard him. "And Bobby Jack computerized the club's sound system. Then there's Jimmy Mission. He's been advertising his stud bull on-line." The last bit of information snagged his attention. Thankfully.

"Jimmy's here?"

"Been running the Mission Ranch for the past year."

"A rancher? *Jimmy?* The last I heard of him, he'd joined the air force and run off to play soldier boy."

"He did that." Her gaze collided with his. "And then he came home."

As if her words hit their mark, he averted her eyes. "So, are you interested in the job?"

She pushed a strand of muddy hair from her eyes. "I already have a job."

He slipped into the old bad-boy Tack with his heartbreaker smile. Devilish delight flashed in his eyes as he leaned over the desk to finger one soiled strap of her ruined dress. "Wrestling pigs? Honey," he drawled, his voice like warm syrup dripping over her favorite blueberry pancakes, "I always had higher aspirations for you."

She leaned back in her chair, away from the warm fingertips playing havoc with her sanity. "For your information," she managed to say, focusing on her irritation rather than the strange sensations stirring in her belly, "I've just covered a historic event. Largest recorded litter in Texas in fifty years."

"The pay's pretty good."

He placed an envelope on her desk, and Annie couldn't help herself. If, *when* a journalism job came through with one of her Top Twenty, she was sure to need extra cash to finance a move. "I can take the pictures at my leisure?"

"As long as I have the prints by close of business on Friday."

"I guess you've got yourself a deal then." He didn't budge, just stared around him and she asked, "Is there anything else?"

"Just looking." He got to his feet and studied the framed articles lining the wall. "Are these yours?"

She nodded, leaning her elbows on the desk, relaxed now that he wasn't stripping her bare with those bluer than blue eyes of his. "Our football team won the state championship last year. Deb's not into sports, so it falls to yours truly."

"These are good—better than good." He indicated a collection of pictures. His attention lingered on one in particular of a young boy walking off the field, the game ball in his hands, victory gleaming in his eyes.

"That was last year's quarterback. He was great. The best we've seen since you took us to a state championship."

His expression eased into a grin. "We had a good team our senior year."

"You pushed the other guys, made them think that a small-town team could really go up against the big-city boys." A smile played at her lips as she remembered the games. She'd stood on the sidelines so many times and watched him, the way he moved, smiled, frowned, yelled, *everything*. "You had a competitive streak even then."

Tack studied a few more pictures. "You're really talented, Annie." The way his gaze shifted to hers, touched her lips, her neck, and lower, she knew he wasn't just talking about her work.

She tried to ignore the sudden change in temperature. "I hope you're right. I'm a jack-of-all-trades here, but the bigger papers employ straight photographers, and that's what I'm after."

"A picture tells a thousand words, huh?" He held her gaze a few seconds more, blue eyes pushing deep, searching, before he turned his attention back to the photographs and gave Annie a chance to study him.

His dark hair and shadowed jaw lent him an air of danger. At the same time, the dimple that cut into one cheek when he smiled softened the edge and gave him a certain charm.

Charm?

She shook away the notion. Focus on his bad habits: his double dose of cockiness, his enormous ego, his rattle-her-nerves smile.

"If all your stuff is this good, you'll land a job soon." He leaned on the corner of her desk, hands resting easily on his thighs. He rubbed his open palms up and down the faded material. An innocent gesture, little more than a habit, but it caught Annie's attention.

She'd always loved his hands. Large and strong, yet oddly gentle. He'd been able to throw a football fifty yards, and pick wildflowers without losing a petal.

His palms continued to stroke up and down the material, the movement a sensual reminder of last night, of those same movements on her back, her buttocks, her belly…

So much for bad habits.

"Annie?"

She licked her lips and tore her gaze away. "Um, yes?"

"I asked how long you've been with the paper."

"Uh, all day." She glanced at her watch. "Speaking of which, I really need to get home."

"I meant, how many years."

"The six since my mother died. Before that, I took care of her and worked odd jobs while I went to school." She grabbed her purse and camera bag.

"We still have something else to talk about." He caught her wrist. The pads of his fingertips pressed against her thudding pulse and heat skittered along her nerve endings.

"Sex," she growled, her senses going into temporary overload. "S-E-X, Tack. Can't you get that through your head?"

"I was thinking more along the lines of a kiss." His hand went to the button of his jeans. A wicked, teasing light flashed in his eyes. "But if you'd rather give up the preliminary round and go straight to the main event—"

"No! Stop!" Her fingers closed over his before she could think better of it. Her thumb brushed the hard ridge straining beneath his jeans and she snatched her hand away as if she'd touched a live wire. "I—I thought you meant we should talk about last night."

"Last night was last night. I'm more interested in tonight. Right now." His gaze held her captive. "I was going to ask you for a kiss."

Her heart launched into overdrive. "No."

"I didn't ask yet."

"Well, I'm saving you the trouble." She took a deep breath. "No." Hell no. Please no. Oh no.

"Why?"

"Because." *Because one kiss might lead to two and two to three and...*

Calm, cool, indifferent.

She forced her gaze from his to glance at her watch, determined to ignore the sudden anticipation that rushed through her veins. "Because I'm late. I have to stop at the hardware store before they close and pick up the new paint for my house."

He eyed her. "Is that the only reason?"

She gave him an innocent look. "Why else?"

"Then this won't take long." His hands came up to cup her face and his lips closed over hers, firm and purposeful, before she had a chance to breathe, much less summon her defenses.

"Open up, honey, and let me in," he murmured against her mouth.

Her lips parted. He was just so close and so warm and he was touching her. Ah, he was touching her.

With firm, hungry lips that slanted so perfectly across her own. With a gently thrusting tongue that probed and stroked and tangled with hers. With strong fingers cradling her cheeks, tilting her face so he could deepen the kiss.

There was none of the old Tack in this kiss. None of the teasing, butterfly pecks a young boy had used to coax an uptight virgin out of her shell so long ago.

This was a man's kiss. Hot, wet and mind-blowing. Intimate. Powerful. *Possessive.*

Realization zapped her, a lightning bolt through the thick fog of desire that blinded her.

What the hell was she doing?

Letting him kiss her. Wanting him to kiss her. Kissing him back— *Oh no!*

She forced herself away and stumbled backward a few steps, gaining some blessed distance.

"That didn't take too long, now, did it?" The words were light, teasing, but there was none of it reflected in his gaze. Bright blue eyes lingered on her lips as if he fought the urge to kiss her again. And again.

"Long enough," she said shakily. *Too long.*

"You look a little unsteady, honey. You all right?"

"Fine," she choked out. Confused. Happy and sad and angry and joyful and—

Calm, cool, indifferent.

Annie gathered her composure, unwilling to let Tack know how deeply he affected her. "I'm *really* late." Her lips tingling, she snatched up her equipment and headed for the door, her steps practiced and sure, despite the pounding of her heart as she walked away.

What she should have done last night.

Breathless moments later, Annie climbed into her battered white Chevy pickup and shoved the keys in the ignition. Her gaze hooked on the sleek, black Harley parked across the street. The urge to climb on, feel the powerful machine vibrate beneath her, hit her hard and fast, and heat speared her body.

But it was nothing compared to the fire that flared, raged deep inside when she saw Tack exit the building, strut toward the motorcycle and straddle the seat. His eyes locked with hers and suddenly it wasn't the machine she wanted to feel beneath her, but him.

"No," she said, gunning the engine. It was one night, and now, one kiss. Annie would be damned if she'd let it turn into something more, if she'd find herself caught in the same trap that had kept her mother chained to a town she hated almost as much as it hated her.

One month, she told herself. Then he would be moving on, out of Annie's life forever.

Until then, she would simply concentrate on finding a new job and fixing up her house, and forget all about Tack Brandon and the fact that he still had her underpants tucked away in his pocket.

TACK SAT on the side of the small twin bed and fingered the silky material. The scent of her filled his nostrils and he got all hot and bothered again. Not that he'd calmed down. Three hours kicking up dust and peeling down a maze of country back roads, and he'd still had a hard-on when he finally climbed off his bike and walked inside the ranch house.

Hell, he didn't even have to see her. Thinking about her was just as powerful, and as frustrating as hell. Because as badly as Tack wanted a repeat of last night, he wanted to know why she'd slept with him in the first place.

He didn't buy her initial story. Annie wasn't a

just sex sort of girl, at least not the Annie he remembered. The Annie who'd blushed and trembled and hidden herself behind ugly sweatshirts and baggy pants.

But this Annie was different. She wore flattering sundresses, looked him straight in the eye and called him out when he damn well deserved it. Her skin was tanned a soft golden hue, and he hadn't once seen her tremble.

But he'd felt her tremble. Last night when she'd been in his arms and he'd been inside her.

Just sex didn't explain her tears, the whisper-soft, "It's been a long time." Nor did it explain the flash of fear in her eyes when he'd kissed her tonight, an expression so quick he would have missed it if he hadn't been paying attention.

But he'd always paid attention where Annie was concerned.

He remembered she'd fancied herself in love with him way back then, though she'd never said the words out loud. He also remembered that the prospect had scared the daylights out of him, and thrilled him at the same time.

Because he'd loved her?

No, but he had felt more for her than he'd ever felt for anyone before. Anyone since.

He'd gone through enough women over the years, prime, experienced, grade-A females, and not one of them had lingered on his mind, or on any other part of his anatomy. Not one.

Only this one.

"Thought you might need an extra blanket." The familiar voice drifted through the crack in the bedroom door, cutting short Tack's thoughts.

He glanced up just as a man entered, a blanket in one arm and a box under the other.

With a crew cut and a baby-smooth face, Eli Sutton looked a hell of a lot different from the long-haired, mustache-wearing wrangler Tack remembered. Eli had been so wild, reckless and carefree back then that Tack had barely noticed the man had fifteen years on him.

He noticed now.

While Eli didn't look a day over his forty-two years, he seemed...tamer. Settled.

Married.

Content.

Eli handed Tack the blanket. "Vera would have come herself—she's been wanting to get up here and say hello—but she don't get around so good with the baby so close to coming. She didn't know if you'd remember where the linens were kept."

"Second shelf, hall closet. A few things haven't changed." His gaze darted to the large shelf filled with sports trophies, from Little League to high school. A half-finished model airplane sat on the corner of a crowded dresser. In the eighth grade he'd started the model as a class project, but he'd never been able to sit still long enough to finish the wings, never been good at anything that kept him chained to a desk or chair. He'd done well in school, but it hadn't come from studying. He had a good memory and he caught on quick, and so he'd pulled in mostly A's and kept a GPA high enough to get him into his father's alma mater, Texas A & M.

The acceptance letter still sat framed on his desk.

"When Vera and I got married and she started cleaning up here, she had me talk to your daddy about packing some of this stuff up into boxes—it's hell to dust all of it—but he said no. Said he wanted a reminder of all you'd given up, all you'd left behind so he could keep on hating you."

Leave it to Eli to speak his mind. "And did he?" Tack asked.

"He tried. He'd come in here every night, but I finally realized it wasn't 'cause he wanted a reminder of why he should hate you, he just wanted a reminder of you. That's why he collected all them videotapes."

He cast a sharp glance at the ranch foreman. "What videotapes?"

"Third shelf in the library. Recorded every one of your races ever televised. He missed you, Tack."

His heart pounded and his chest tightened before he could fight back the feeling, the hope. "He never picked up the phone."

"And neither did you."

But I came close. So close.

The clock ticked away a full minute as both men stood there. Finally, Eli seemed to remember something. He pulled the box from under his arm and handed it to Tack. "Me and the boys got you a little welcome-home present. Thought you could use it."

Tack opened the box and saw a straw Resistol sitting inside.

"It ain't the same one you used to wear, mind

you—that thing died a long time ago. But it looks like it."

He couldn't help the grin that spread across his face. "I wore that hat every summer from the time I turned thirteen to the night I..." *Left*. The word caught in the sudden tightness in his throat and his mouth drew into a thin line. "Thanks, Eli, but I won't be needing it."

"I figured that. Rumor has it you're selling."

Tack put the hat back into the box. "Good news travels fast."

"It ain't such good news, but it don't come as much of a surprise. Bets had it that you wouldn't even make it home, much less stick around. Some boys lost a hell of a lot of money when you showed up."

"What about you?"

Eli grinned. "I made enough to buy Vera that cradle she's been wanting." When Tack tried to hand him back the hatbox, he shook his head. "You hold on to that. You never know when it might come in handy."

TACK REPLAYED the conversation with Eli as he stripped off his shirt and stretched out on the bed.

No, he'd never called his father, but he'd thought about it. Thought about picking up the phone and calling to hear Coop's voice. Then he'd think about what his old man would say.

Ain't nothing more important than this land.

If you walk away, don't bother coming back.

You ain't welcome—

Stop it! The past was over and done with.

Forget. *Focus*.

He clamped his eyes shut, but try as he might, he couldn't seem to clear his head, to think about the next training session, the next race.

His eyes opened, drinking in the display of trophies, the knickknacks, the hatbox—all reminders of the life he'd left behind.

Climbing from the bed, he pulled on his jeans, snatched up a blanket and headed outside. For some cool air. Some freedom. Some blessed distance.

From the past.

From the present.

He ended up down by the creek, watching the play of moonlight on the mirrorlike surface, listening to the trickle of water and the buzz of insects. The sounds pushed inside his head and shoved aside Eli's voice, his father's, everything except the soft, sweet whisper of water.

He stretched out on his back and stared up at the sky, but he didn't see the stars or the moon. He saw her. A halo of silver hair framing the sweetest, warmest woman he'd ever had the pleasure of sinking into.

She'd fueled his dreams for so long, made him toss and turn and swell until he was rock-hard and desperate for release. Even when he'd slept with other women, Annie had always been there, living in his memories, a shining ray in his stormy past.

However persistent, she'd always been a dream. A nighttime reprieve from life on the road, the stress of going from race to race and keeping himself primed and pumped and focused.

Not anymore.

He was wide-awake now, and she was right in front of him. Not the same soft, sweet girl who'd lingered in his head all this time, but a woman, her features sharp and defined rather than fogged by time and a young boy's memory. *Real.*

He felt her quivering and needy in his arms. Heard her tiny, high-pitched whimpers. Saw the fine sheen of sweat covering her shoulders and breasts. Smelled the steamy heat and the faint scent of peaches that clung to her naked body.

The blood rushed through his veins, surging straight to his groin...

He couldn't stop thinking about her, but not just about the way she'd felt surrounding him, riding him, but about the tremble of her voice when she'd whispered in his ear, the warmth of her tears on his skin, the way she'd touched her lips to the pounding of his pulse, as if she could feel, taste the life pumping through his veins. As if she wanted to.

Those lips at his throat. That's what he couldn't forget.

What he wanted to feel again.

He would. As many times as necessary to slake the lust eating at his common sense. As intent as Tack was on selling the Big B, he was suddenly just as determined to purge himself of the beautiful Miss Annie.

This time when he left Inspiration—for the last time—he would be rid of the dream that had haunted him all these years. He could make a clean break, no lingering memories. No regrets.

He had to work Annie Divine out of his system.

And that meant he had to get her back into his bed.

6

"TELL ME *EVERYTHING*," Deb demanded the minute Annie picked up the phone early Sunday morning.

"Good morning to you, too."

"The man has your panties, for Pete's sake, and you didn't tell dear old Deb."

"No, no, you didn't wake me. I've been up for hours. What's new with me? Well, my roof sprung a new leak after last night's rain and my air conditioner's still out."

"Okay, it's five in the morning, I shouldn't have called so early— Bless my Gucci-loving soul, he isn't there, is he? Because I may be insensitive, but if I interrrupted the two of you while you were—"

"It's just me and the twins." A loud clatter drifted from outside and she added, "And Mrs. Pope."

"You have to get a life, Annie. Sleeping with two collie puppies isn't my idea of a hot Saturday night—*Mrs. Pope?* The old lady's in bed with you?"

"She's in her side garden, about thirty feet from my bedroom window, making enough racket with her gardening tools that she might as well be in bed with me."

"Gardening at five in the morning?"

"More like revenge." Tools clattered and Mrs. Pope launched into her fourth chorus of "Amazing Grace." "She's mad at me because I was up late stripping my kitchen floor a few nights ago and had all the lights in the house blazing. She said the glare kept the entire neighborhood awake."

"She's the only neighbor you've got for two miles."

"She also wants me to reimburse her seven dollars or she's going to report me for disturbing the peace."

"Why seven dollars?"

"She went to bingo early the next morning and lost seven dollars because she was tired."

"Bingo isn't about skill. It's about luck."

"That's why I gave her a copy of *Bingo for Bucks*."

"Was she appreciative?"

"I don't think so. I can hear her hooking up the sprinklers." Annie crawled out of bed and reached the window just as a shower of spray splattered her. "Ugh," she sputtered and shoved the window down.

"What's wrong?"

"I'm all wet."

"Speaking of wet, tell me *everything* that happened after I left last night."

"You're shameless, and nothing happened." Her lips tingled at the memory and she stiffened. *Calm, cool, indifferent.* "We spent one night together, and it's over. I don't see what the big deal is. It wasn't even an entire night. Just a few hours."

"Hours?" Excitement bubbled in Deb's voice. "I heard athletes had stamina, but *hours?* Where can I get one?" Annie tried to ignore the niggling anger when she thought of Deb "getting one." Or more importantly, when she thought of Deb getting Tack.

Jealousy?

She shook away the notion. Before Deb could ask another question, she added, "I've got a leaky roof to fix. See you at work tomorrow," and punched the disconnect button on her cordless.

She showered, donned a pair of shorts and a tank top and pulled her hair back into a ponytail. Then she ushered the twins out the front door to do their business. Grabbing a red ball, she walked to the edge of the front porch, pitched the toy into a batch of bluebonnets in Mrs. Pope's front garden. The twins scurried after the ball and Annie headed back inside.

She managed two steps before she heard Mrs. Pope shriek at the top of her lungs.

"Annie Divine! Those mongrels pooped in my flower bed!"

Annie leaned out the front door and smiled. "Then I guess we're even."

"Even? How do you figure that?"

"Do you know how much fertilizer costs at the feed store? At least double what you lost at bingo. But seeing as how we're neighbors, I'll call it even. By the way, how did you like the book?"

Annie ducked back inside seconds before a spray of water splattered the screen door where she'd been standing. She chuckled. Never a dull moment.

Taking a deep breath, she turned to her next order of business—fixing the oval-shaped spot marring the already cracked living-room ceiling. Her gaze dropped to survey the room, from an old worn sofa and chair, a scarred coffee table, to the far corner where she stored tripods and several camera cases. The entire place needed an overhaul—from the chipped and peeling outside, to the inside—if she ever intended to get a decent offer when she put it up for sale.

But first things first…

She took a deep breath and moved the sofa out of the way, then the coffee table. Her elbow bumped an old pink embroidered photo album that sat on top and sent it sailing to the ground. She spent the next few minutes gathering pictures and placing them back inside. Her gaze traveled over photos of herself as a child, the house, Coop—everything Cherry Divine had loved in her life.

Annie's gaze lingered on a prom photo she'd taken with Tack. He smiled back at the camera and her chest tightened.

She steeled herself against the feeling and shut the album. One month, she told herself as she placed the book back in its spot. Then Tack Brandon would be leaving.

If only that thought didn't bother her almost as much as the idea of him staying.

"SHE'S A WILD ONE. Fern won't let not a one of the men around here touch her, much less take a ride."

Tack stood next to Eli just after sunup and stared across the corral at a dark brown horse. "She looks tame enough."

"Looks can be deceiving. I broke many a horse in my day. Been in charge of the breeding stock here for your daddy going on twenty years now, but this one's got me by the balls. Coop actually got close enough to stroke her once, but I ain't had the same luck." Eli shrugged. "I suggested using her as a broodmare, but you know old Coop. He always loved a good challenge. Wasn't about to give up on this one without a fight."

Bones chose that moment to bark, effectively killing the subject before Tack did it himself. "Come on, boy." Tack slapped his thigh and Bones came running up.

"That the mutt Effie was hollering about yesterday?"

Tack stroked the dog's shiny coat. "One and the same. He spent the night at the vet and had a thorough checkup. He's a little lean, but healthy." Tack eyed Eli. "Those boys of yours like dogs?"

"Too much for their own good." Eli grinned. "I'll tell you what, I'd be willing to take this dog off your hands if you'll ride fence with Bart for me this morning. That'll give me a chance to take Bones here home and get him settled in."

"And?"

Eli looked sheepish. "Drive Vera to church. She's too big to fit behind the wheel of that little car of hers, and she ain't very good at driving my truck. I used to drive her and the boys while Coop did fence duty, but with him passing on this past week, we're a man short—"

"Go," Tack cut in, giving Bones one last rub.

"You sure?"

"I haven't set a saddle in a long time. But I'll do my best." Tack turned and headed for the barn.

"Just remember," Eli called after him, a chuckle warming his voice, "it's like making love. Once you take a good ride, you never forget how."

IT WAS THE BEST RIDE he'd had in a hell of a long time.

Tack kneed the quarter horse and raced over the open pasture, leaving Bart working on a stretch of barbed wire while he headed down the fence to mend a break he'd spotted earlier. The sun blazed, sending drops of sweat trickling between his shoulder blades. The wind whipped at his face. The motion of the horse worked his thigh muscles, drawing a steady, throbbing ache.

Tack loved every second.

He didn't even mind the work itself. With a boot top of staples and a hammer, he threw himself into the tedious chore of stretching loose fence and hammering it back into place, grateful for something to do besides think about his father or the ranch. Or Annie and her starring role in last night's fantasy.

He could still see her as she'd been in his thoughts, his memories. Waist deep in the river, her breasts wet and glorious in the moonlight, her nipples dark, puckered tips begging for his mouth... *Man, oh, man, you got it bad—*

Focus!

He concentrated on the hammer in his hand and spent the rest of the day working himself into exhaustion. The sun inched below the horizon by the time he rode back to the house, sore and tired. At the same time, his muscles tingled and his nerves twitched with awareness. He felt invigorated. Alive. The way he felt after a good race or a rigorous training session.

Or a hard day cowboying.

Not that the feeling would last. It was his first day back in the saddle. Once the newness wore off, so would the pleasure. Then he would start to feel stifled, trapped. Just like before.

A loud bark drew Tack's attention and he turned to see Bones jump off the back porch of the house and run toward him.

"What happened?" he asked Eli, who followed the dog. "The kids didn't like Bones?"

"They were crazy about him. It was Vera. And it wasn't Bones, specifically. More like his eating habits. He ate an entire apple pie meant for the church bake sale and half a Bundt cake. Vera was mad as a hornet and told me to bring him back to you." He shrugged. "Sorry, man. Hey—" his face brightened "— Bart's got a little girl and his wife likes dogs—got one of her own. I could ask him to help you out."

"I'd appreciate it."

Eli took Bones and headed to the bunkhouse to catch Bart before he went home, and Tack started for the house. His gaze snagged on Fern and he found himself backtracking to the corral.

Wild or not, she was still beautiful. One of the

finest horses he'd ever seen. Glossy brown coat. Strong hind legs. Intelligent eyes.

He wasn't sure what drew him, but he found himself unhooking the latch and slipping inside the corral before he could think better of it. He wasn't a cowboy, but a dirt-bike racer, and he was as far out of his element as a man could get.

The animal glanced at him and he saw a flicker of apprehension before it disappeared in the black depths of her eyes. Muscles rippled and tensed beneath her sleek coat. Tack took a step closer. The walk, the approach, came back to him in a rush and he remembered sitting on the fence, watching his father soothe a new gelding.

The animal snorted a warning, but Tack was careful, sure, as he reached out. Soft, silky horse-hair met his callused palm. Surprisingly, the animal didn't bolt. Ten years faded away and he was eighteen again, soothing his own horse, a prized Arabian his father had purchased as a graduation present.

Cooper Brandon had always had an eye for beauty, and a hankering for a good challenge—

Over and done with, he told himself again. *Forget and focus.*

He shifted his attention back to the horse, to the soft feel of hair beneath his palm. Another stroke and the animal trembled. "Don't worry, girl. You're safe with me. I'd rather bust my balls on metal than horseflesh." He said the words, but his hand lingered a few seconds on the animal's mane.

Tack forced himself away, toward the house for a shower and some supper before he headed back outside for another night of freedom beneath the stars. Like the horse, Tack Brandon had a wild streak of his own. He'd lived too many years under his father's stifling rule. Now he craved air and space and distance from any and everything, especially the house filled with so many reminders.

The fantasies were another matter altogether. Those he welcomed the moment he closed his eyes.

ANNIE WAS NOT GOING to look.

No matter how perfectly the first light of day spilled through the trees and sculpted the man standing between two big cedars not more than ten yards away.

No matter how the surrounding foliage cast just the right amount of shadow to accent the corded muscles of his shoulders and arms.

No matter how bronze and beautiful and *naked* he was... Well, almost.

His back to her as he stared out over the crystal creek bed, he wore a pair of snug, faded jeans, but instead of camouflaging what lay beneath, they molded the shape of his buttocks, his lean hips and strong thighs. A rip in the denim bisected his right thigh, giving her a peek at silky dark hair and tanned skin.

She sighted through the lens, moved a half inch this way, a fraction that way. Closer to find just the right angle... *No!*

Her finger stalled just shy of the shutter, her hand tightened on the camera. What was she doing? She was supposed to be taking pictures of the ranch. She'd purposely dragged herself out of bed before daybreak, knowing the light would be just right to shoot without a flash and portray the quiet serenity of a Texas sunrise at the Big B. The less she had to use flashes or strobes, the more *real* her pictures. Tack might want a few photos, but she always sought to tell a story with her work, even if the pictures were only meant as a sales tool.

She intended to show the natural charm of a winding creek lined with cypress and cedar trees, the breathtaking quality of the hills, the strength of the land. Not to snap pictures of the bare-chested owner with a tantalizing rip in his too-tight jeans—

The thought stalled as Tack reached overhead to stretch. Muscles rippled. Shadows chased sunlight across his bare torso and the air lodged in her throat.

If a picture told a story, Tack's was certain to be a triple-X feature. It was just a casual stretch, yet everything about the movement screamed *sex*. From the sensual arch of his back, his hips thrust out just enough to emphasize the bulge beneath his zippered fly, to the stroke of long, lean fingers through his dark, sun-kissed hair.

She stared at the image in the viewfinder, unable to tear her gaze away, to get while the getting was good. She should go back to her truck, get her tripod and large-format camera and do some panoramic shots from the top of Brandon Bluff. At least the morning wouldn't be a total waste. The creek shots she could get later. Much later, after Tack Brandon was gone and Annie Divine wasn't so fresh from a night of tossing and turning and thinking about him.

Wanting him.

He turned, giving her his profile as he reached up and picked a peach from a nearby tree. She watched as he dusted the fruit off on his jeans and bit into the pale flesh. Juice spurted, trailing over his tanned fingers, dripping down his muscled forearm.

Annie couldn't help herself. Her trigger finger itched. The shutter clicked.

Tack stopped chewing for a fraction of a second and she froze. He'd heard. She knew it. She was too close, the sound too pronounced in the hushed morning. She lowered the camera, bracing herself for a confrontation.

He didn't turn toward her. He simply stood there for a long, drawn-out moment. Then his mouth moved, his stubble-covered jaw worked at the fruit again, as if he was unaware of her presence.

That, or he was ignoring her.

No. Tack wasn't a man to look the other way, not when he wanted something, and he wanted her. He'd made no secret that he'd like a repeat performance of their night together.

He had no clue she was there.

What harm could it do to take a few pictures? It was the touching she had trouble with. Letting her guard slip and pushing her fears to the back burner, Annie indulged herself. Just this once.

Raising the camera, she sighted him again, following his every movement through the viewfinder. His teeth sinking into the soft pulp, the decadent spurt of juice over his tanned skin.

He abandoned the peach to catch a trickle of sweetness along the inside of his forearm. The tip of his tongue caught a golden drop before gliding up along his smooth skin, and Annie's heart stalled.

Heat flooded between her legs as she remembered his touch. The wet flick of his tongue on the inside of her thigh.

A last, lingering lick at the tender side of his wrist and Annie's knees trembled.

He took another bite, lips working at the flesh, teeth nibbling, and Annie's body responded once more. To the sight, the sound, the memory of his hungry mouth feasting on her the way he feasted on the peach.

There was something about Tack that stoked the passionate fire deep inside her, fed the flames until they blazed hot and bright. Consuming. He drew a physical response from her that was unlike anything she'd ever experienced.

Physical. She focused on the thought, intent on keeping her emotions separate. Protected. Buried.

He sank his teeth deeper into the succulent fruit. Her breathing grew harsh, her heart drummed a frantic tempo. The camera slipped from her grasp and stopped at her waist, anchored by the strap around her neck. The firm edge of the canvas grazed one throbbing nipple and she gasped. The sound echoed in her ears, thundering through the silence separating them.

Tack didn't so much as flinch, much less turn accusing eyes on her. He took his last bite of peach, pitched the core and licked his fingers, and Annie felt her first spasm. A soft clenching that made her entire body vibrate as it worked its way from between her legs, spreading through her the way the peach juice had drenched Tack's lean fingers.

By the time he'd licked the last one clean, she'd managed to catch her breath. But she couldn't move. She leaned against the tree, quivering and spent and still needy. While she'd had an orgasm, it wasn't enough to quiet the hunger inside her. She'd had a taste, or rather, he'd had the taste and she'd felt it, and now she wanted to feel more.

To feel him.

Closing her eyes, she fought to summon her defenses and pull herself together. She had a few yards on him. If she bolted, she could get away before he walked toward her, touched her, and she lost what little resistance she had.

Resistance? She was this close to falling at his feet and begging him to make love to her. But it wasn't the sex act itself that posed the threat. It was the begging. The *need*. The last thing Annie wanted was to need Tack Brandon, to crave more than a few moments of carnal bliss to the point that she stopped thinking of herself and wanted only him.

She stiffened and her eyes snapped open. She would not fall for Tack all over again, not without a fight. No matter how fierce the attraction—

He was gone.

She stared at the empty patch of grass and disappointment crept through her, followed by a rush of relief. He really hadn't seen her.

Snatching up her camera bag, she forced her legs to move back down the path to her truck. He might have reduced her to a quivering mass of hormones, but at least he wasn't aware of it, and that meant he had no idea how he affected her. Annie intended to keep it that way, to keep her precious control. Over her life, her destiny. Her dreams.

Now if she could just add her traitorous body to the list.

TACK WAS THIS CLOSE to going up in flames by the time he made it back to the ranch house and his old bedroom. He could still see Annie, leaning back against the tree, her breasts heaving, erect nipples outlined by the thin fabric of her pale pink blouse.

God, he wanted to be inside her, and she wanted him there. He knew it. She'd been so absorbed in what she was feeling, she hadn't even realized he'd been looking at her. He'd seen the desire on her face when he'd licked away the last of the peach.

The sweetness lingered on his tongue and a bolt of heat shot straight to his already throbbing erection. He slid the button of his jeans free and eased the zipper down enough to give himself some much-needed room. Man, he was hard. *Hungry.*

For more than a piece of fruit. He wanted the real thing. *Her.* Five long strides and he could have had it.

Annie. Beneath him. Surrounding him. Sending him to heaven.

Not yet.

Not until he figured out what she was all about. He wasn't pushing inside her sweet body until he'd managed to push inside her pretty little head and get some real answers.

In the meantime...

Tack walked into the bathroom, twisted the cold-water knob and started to push his jeans and underwear down. A door slammed somewhere in the house and an angry shout carried down the hallway.

"Tack Brandon! I've got a bone to pick with you."

Yanking up his jeans, he grimaced as the fabric fit tightly over his throbbing length. Man, oh, man, he had it real bad.

"Tack Brandon!" The voice echoed louder. Closer.

He reached the bedroom doorway just as a large woman, salt-and-pepper hair pulled back in a bun, rounded the corner, carrying Bones.

"Don't tell me. You must be Bart's wife."

She frowned, her round, pudgy face pinched into a frown. "And you're the sorry SOB who sent this mongrel home with my husband." She plopped Bones on the ground and dusted dog hair off her neon-blue housedress.

"What did he do?"

"Ate three loaves of my pumpkin bread, but that's beside the point. This poor excuse for a stud was putting major moves on my Camille."

"Camille?"

"My prizewinning poodle. She was enjoying her favorite biscuit when this mutt corners her in my kitchen. She's whimpering and crying when I come in and see you-know-who about to...to..." The woman colored and waved a hand in Bones's direction. "Well, you get the idea."

Tack shifted his stance to give his crotch a little more room. Unfortunately, he got the idea all too well.

"Anyhow," the woman went on, "it took a rolled newspaper over his head and a lot of tugging and pulling to get him away from her."

"Maybe she's in heat."

"Not my sweet little Camille!"

"Sounds like a possibility, if you ask me. Poor Bones here is a healthy male. He's got needs. This Camille's obviously got needs."

"I will not have Camille breeding with every two-bit Casanova that sniffs in her direction, nor will I have this sack of bones raiding my pumpkin bread." She turned on her heel and stormed down the hallway. The front door slammed shut and Tack's accusing gaze dropped to Bones.

"Looks like you just got yourself kicked out of home number two." Bones's tail thumped enthusiastically and Tack shook his head. "I know it's not all your fault, but you have to behave yourself, Bones, or we'll never find a place for you. That means staying out of the kitchen." Bones barked, and Tack added, "I know, I know. It wasn't just the food you were after this time, but you still need to learn some self-control."

He walked back into the bathroom, pulled off his jeans and briefs, wincing as the material grazed the hard evidence of his own lack of self-control. Thankfully, Bart's wife had been too mad to notice, otherwise, she'd have taken a newspaper to Tack for sure. A Sunday edition, by the size of things.

The dog whimpered, and Tack turned to see Bones had followed him into the bathroom. The dog's mouth hung open, tongue lolling to the side as he panted from the morning heat. That, or he was still worked up over Camille.

"I know the feeling, buddy." Tack turned on the spray, stepped into the shower and let the cold tame his eager body. "I know the feeling all too well."

"WHAT'S WRONG WITH YOU?" Deb asked Wednesday morning when Annie walked into the newspaper office.

"What do you mean?" She flipped on her computer and stowed her camera bag and purse beneath her desk.

"You look flushed. Are you coming down with something?"

"No." Just a bad case of stupidity, Annie thought as she pulled out her notes on the luncheon she'd covered yesterday and tried to still her pounding heart.

Pounding, even after twenty minutes, an ice-cold diet soda and a drive into town with the truck's air conditioner blasting. But nothing short of a dip into a river of ice cubes could have lowered her body temperature after another early-morning down by Brandon Creek.

Her third to be exact.

She should have known he'd be there. She *had* known. After spotting him again on the second morning, she'd known as soon as she walked down the path that she'd find him at the same place. Looking as sexy as ever in worn jeans and nothing else. Nothing but a peach in his hand.

The second two days had been a repeat of the first morning. Tack devouring the fruit, licking his hunger away while Annie watched him. *Felt* him.

She flipped open her notebook and noted the tremble of her fingers, the strange tingling of her skin. For all her disapointment that she'd given in to her baser desires again, she felt oddly exhilarated. Reckless. Daring. The way she'd felt when she'd walked around wearing her first pair of skimpy lace panties.

After a lifetime of nice, conservative granny panties, as her mom had called them, Annie had bought a pair of French-cut bikinis the day she'd enrolled in college. She'd been celebrating the start of her new life away from Inspiration.

Things had changed a few days later. Her mother had been diagnosed with cancer and Annie had made the decision to commute to the University of Texas and live at home to tend Cherry.

As disappointed as Annie had been, she always remembered that first day walking around Austin wearing her new, sexy lingerie. No one had known, but she had, and it had made her feel good about herself.

The way she'd felt this morning, taking her pleasure and not fearing for her peace of mind at the same time. Tack had been oblivious, far away from touching her and stirring the emotions simmering deep down inside, and Annie had been…on fire.

If only it was enough.

She ignored the thought and fanned herself with the edge of the notebook.

"You're definitely coming down with something." Deb took a sip from her newest mug, Ballbuster And Proud Of It. "Maybe you've got a fever."

"I'm fine, Mom."

"I am not acting like a mother."

"Oops, I said the three-letter word."

"It's not that I have anything against mothers," Deb said, "except my own, which is why I have no desire to squeeze out a little bundle of joy anytime soon."

"Bad parenting isn't genetic, you know."

"And poor choices aren't either," Deb said.

"What's that supposed to mean?"

"Just because your mother had a miserable love life, doesn't mean you're doomed to the same. Live a little, Annie, and stop worrying about making the same mistakes Cherry made. Tack Brandon's the best-looking cowboy I've seen in a long time."

"He's not a cowboy." Annie braced herself for a barrage of questions, but Deb simply sipped her coffee and walked back over to her own desk.

"By the way, I've got to drive to Austin, so I need you to cover the This Is Your Neighbor for this edition."

"I can get to it after I finish this piece on the weekly seniors luncheon. So who is it this week? I hope it's Granny Baines. She kept hinting about it through lunch yesterday." Granny Baines was one of the few older citizens of Inspiration who didn't look down her nose at Annie. While she hadn't approved of Cherry, she'd always treated Annie decently.

Of course, she also wanted to get her picture in the paper.

"It's not Granny Baines," Deb said. "It's a he."

Annie arched an eyebrow at her editor. "And you're not covering it? He must be too old to qualify as hunk material. That or married."

"Neither."

"Young and single? Are you sure you're not the one who's coming down with something?"

"The fact of the matter is, Mr. Young and Single requested you."

"Me?" Her eyes narrowed. "Who is it?"

"Your gusto-grabbing cowboy."

"Oh no." Dread churned fast and furious in Annie's stomach and she groaned. "On second thought, I think I am feeling sick."

"A touch of flu?"

Annie shook her head. "Too many peaches."

7

ANNIE GRIPPED her notebook and camera bag,
rang the doorbell and ignored the urge to bolt.

"It's just an interview," she told herself for the
hundredth time since Deb had dropped the
bomb. It *was* just an interview, despite what had
happened between them.

"Just stay calm," she muttered. "Calm and cool
and indifferent—"

"Indifferent to what, honey?"

The deep voice brought her whirling around to
see Tack clad in nothing but a pair of jeans, a
white towel hooked around the strong column of
his neck. Drops of water slid down his deeply
bronzed shoulders and arms to bead in the black
mat of chest hair that stretched from nipple to
nipple. The forest of ebony thinned and narrowed
to a silky funnel that bisected his washboard
stomach and disappeared between the gaping
waistband of his unbuttoned jeans. Annie's gaze
lingered on the hard ridge beneath the zipper.

"Cold showers aren't what they used to be."

Her gaze snapped up at the sound of his voice.
"W-what?"

He grinned, a sexy slant to his lips that made
Annie's heart stop for a long moment. "I said, a
cold shower isn't enough to beat this heat."

Annie wiped a trail of perspiration from her forehead. "The weatherman said we're headed for a record-breaking day. Ninety-eight degrees."

He winked. "I wasn't talking about the temperature outside, honey." He scrubbed at his damp hair with the towel. "And you didn't answer my question. Indifferent to what?"

You. The word rushed through her thoughts and straight to her lips where she bit it back. Annie couldn't help the strange emotions stirring deep inside, but she could keep them contained. Controlled.

She took a deep breath. "To the heat," she said matter-of-factly. "Calm, cool and indifferent. The only way to cope with a Texas summer." She wiped another trail of sweat from her temple. "So where do you want to do it?" She indicated her notebook. "I've got a tight schedule today—a luncheon at city hall and a follow-up on Tess Johnson's litter—so if we could hurry this up, I would really appreciate it."

He stepped back. "How about the kitchen?"

"Fine," she said as she slipped past him. Her shoulder brushed against one muscular arm and heat zigzagged down her arm to make her fingers tingle. She managed a calm voice. "I can find my own way while you finish dressing."

"Sure thing." Two strong fingers slid the button of his jeans into place and he grinned. "All done."

"What about a shirt?"

"I'm pretty comfortable the way I am, but if it bothers you..." Blue eyes drilled into her. "Does it bother you?"

Yes! She shrugged. "Suit yourself."

"I intend to, honey," he murmured as she turned to precede him into the house. "I surely do."

Minutes later, Annie sat at the kitchen table sipping a diet soda while Tack stood at the counter and poured a glass of iced tea.

"Let's see…" She studied several pages of the notebook and tried to calm her pounding heart. "You'll have to give me a second to find the questions. Deb's got the handwriting of a serial killer and she does all the interviews for this column, except the one with Jimmy Mission." At his questioning glance, she added, "They don't get along too well."

"A woman exists that Jimmy doesn't get along with?" Tack dropped two spoonfuls of sugar into his tea and stirred.

"Deb's not your normal woman. She's got…attitude."

"You mean balls."

"That's what Jimmy told her."

He sipped the tea and added two more heaping spoonfuls. "It's no wonder they dislike each other."

"I think *hate* would be a better word. Jimmy volunteered for the dunking booth last year at the annual spring carnival—"

"Are we talking about the same Jimmy who won't go within a stone's throw of the river?"

"The one and only. The mayor persuaded him by saying that it was a shallow tank and Jimmy probably wouldn't even get wet since the girls' baseball team was on a seven-year losing streak and all the boys would be at the kissing booth with Mary Jo Madden—she was the Southwest Rodeo Queen. Mostly, Jimmy was supposed to sit up there, bare-chested, while the girls oohed and aahed and forked over a buck to make themselves look charitable. He didn't count on Deb seeking revenge for the balls statement, or the fact that she grew up with three jock brothers."

He chuckled. "She dunked him?"

"Seventy-two times. It was the highlight of the carnival. That and the yelling match that used so many four-letter words the church ladies called an emergency prayer meeting right there on the spot. Deb and Jimmy haven't spoken since..." Her words faded as she watched him dunk two more spoonfuls of sugar. "Why don't you just add a few ice cubes to the sugar bowl?"

He grinned. "What can I say? I've got a sweet tooth."

It wasn't his words so much as the gleam in his blue eyes that made her think of long dark nights and tangled sheets and lots of sweet, sweet heat.

"What about you, honey? You like sweets?"

Yes. She fixed her gaze on the notebook. "On occasion. Question number one. Occupation?"

Tack turned a kitchen chair, straddled it and rested his forearms on the back, the ice-cold glass cradled in his palms. "Professional motocross racer. Eight years riding pro. I started out working as a mechanic in a motorcycle shop after I left here. The owner raced as a hobby and he showed me the ropes. I started my first pro season a year later. So you've been with the *In Touch* how long now?"

She penciled his answer down. "Six years."

"And before that?"

"I worked my way through college. I've got a bachelor's in journalism and a minor in communications. Now, on to the next—"

"A bachelor's?" he cut in. "You couldn't do that at Grant County Community College."

"I didn't. I went to the University of Texas."

"I thought you stayed home and took care of your mother?"

"I did," she said tightly. "I commuted. Now, about the second question—"

"But that's a two-hour drive each way."

"I scheduled all of my classes on Tuesdays and Thursdays and took six years to get a four-year degree."

Tack thought of sweet, shy Annie driving hours on end, burying her head in schoolbooks, hanging in there and staying focused while her classmates lived on campus, went to parties and football games. Warmth swelled in his chest. "You wanted a degree that bad?"

"Yes," she said through clenched teeth before giving him a pointed stare. "This is your interview."

"Annie, Annie," he clucked. "You need to relax. Don't be so uptight. I'm just curious to know what you've been up to all these years."

"I am not uptight."

"Then you must be nervous." He took a long gulp of iced tea and watched the way her gaze riveted on his mouth. "Do I make you nervous, honey?"

"Of course not." Her words were so cool, so

matter-of-fact, he almost bought her indifference, except for the white-knuckled grip she had on the pencil.

As if she noticed the direction of his gaze, she relaxed her hand. "I'm just pressed for time, that's all. So what about you? Did you make it to college?"

He shook his head, his grin fading as he thought of those early years. "I was busy surviving. When I left home, things were tight. I could barely feed myself, much less pay for school."

"What about that football scholarship to Texas A & M? You could have played college ball, all expenses paid and gotten an education in the process."

"I thought about it. Hell, I even came close to driving up to College Station. I really liked playing football. But not enough to go head-to-head with guys who loved the game. I only played high school ball to get away from the ranch. Once I was on my own, I didn't need a way out anymore. I lost my drive."

Her green eyes caught flecks of sunlight as her gaze rose to meet his. "But you found it again with motorcycle racing."

"I was the hungriest rookie to ever hit the track."

"And now?"

He thought of the contracts tucked away in his duffle bag, still unsigned, and shrugged. "I'm still hungry, but I'm getting older. Most of the guys coming into the circuit are young, eighteen and nineteen. Talented kids like Jeff Emig, Jeremy McGrath, Ezra Lusk. I've got nearly ten years on all of them." He took a long drink of iced tea and grinned. "The competition is tough, but it makes winning all the sweeter, and you know I like sweets."

A smile played at her lips. "Still a sucker for a challenge?"

"Yeah, I am," he said, his thoughts shifting from racing to Annie. A grown-up, voluptuous Annie standing near the creek bed, her lashes at half-mast, her lips parted, a soft sigh quivering from her throat. Heat fired his blood and his gaze captured hers. "When it comes to something I really want."

The tension coiled thick between them for several long moments as Tack let the meaning of his words sink in.

"What is it you really—" Her question faded into a series of loud barks as Bones bounced through the doorway to beg at Tack's feet. "I—I think the dog must be hungry," she blurted, as if she'd just realized what she'd been about to ask.

"He's always hungry." Tack glared at Bones, got to his feet and retrieved a can of dog food from a nearby cabinet.

"This is your dog?"

He shook his head as he opened the can and poured it into a bowl. "A stray I picked up at Effie's. I call him Bones."

"For such a skinny dog, he sure likes to eat," she pointed out as Bones started lapping up the dog food.

"There's no like about it. He loves to eat." Tack returned to his seat. "Come to think of it, so do I." He reached into the fruit bowl at the center of the table and grabbed a peach. "How about you, honey? You hungry?"

Annie stiffened and shook her head, her gaze riveted on the piece of fruit.

He cast her a sly grin. "And here I thought you liked peaches."

Worry lit her eyes, and by her erect posture he knew she was bracing herself, fully expecting him to call her out about her harmless voyeurism. To tease her. Hell, he was half tempted just to see if she would turn that enticing shade of pink he remembered so well.

As much as he liked to see her blush, he wouldn't break the connection her simple act had forged between them. The small thread of trust. For the first time, Annie had taken the initiative. She'd taken her pleasure as bold and brave as you please, revealing how much she had changed.

And he liked it.

He'd always had to coax the smallest kisses from her, charm her out of those big baggy clothes. She'd never been comfortable with her luscious body, afraid people would think she resembled Cherry in more ways than appearance. She'd never initiated a kiss, never been daring or flirty like the other girls who'd pursued him back in high school.

At the time, Annie had been a breath of fresh air. Pretty and sweet. As appealing and challenging as that innocence had been, Tack wasn't interested in picking up where they'd left off. The hunter and his prey.

He wanted an equal partner this time. A *woman*. One just as bold as she was shy, as greedy as she was giving. One who burned as fiercely as he did and didn't try to hide her desire.

He wanted the sexy woman his sweet little Annie had become.

The sun filtered through the kitchen windows, bathing them in a warm glow that drew a line of perspiration from her temple, despite the cold air blowing from the air-conditioning vents.

"You hot, honey?"

"It's a little warm in here, but bearable," she replied in a cool, calm voice. So damn calm. "My notes say that you've won eight national motocross championships, and have raced for Suzuki, Honda and Yamaha. So where's home base? Coop said something about California."

As always, the mention of his father sliced through him like a dull razor, dicing his thoughts. He cast her a sharp glance. "He knew where I was living?"

"He kept up."

A strange sense of hope surged deep inside, but he forced the feeling back down and shrugged. "Yeah, I guess he did. It wasn't as if he had to go to any trouble. Just tune in to the latest sports channel and watch a postrace interview."

"Or maybe he kept tabs on you—"

"Can we get back to the interview?" he cut in, determined to change the subject, to ignore the hurt, stay one step ahead of it for as long as possible.

Forever.

She stared at him, her green gaze searching, comforting. Understanding lit her eyes and Tack glimpsed the old Annie. The one who'd listened

and comforted whenever he'd been mad at Coop.
As much as he wanted the woman she'd become,
it gave him an odd sense of peace to know a little
of the old Annie remained. The friend she'd been
before she'd been his lover.

At that moment, he wanted to sit with her, gaze
at her, talk to her even more than he wanted to
take her to bed.

As if she sensed his thoughts, her eyes
dropped, breaking the spell as she glanced at the
pad. "Where in California?"

"Encino. I've got a little place near the track
where I do laps. So, honey—" he took a bite out of
his peach and winked at her, comfortable now to
be back on track, focused on the present, rather
than on his damnable past "—you work all day
and go home to an empty house?"

"Yes and no." She plowed into the next question as if to stay focused herself. "Now, about
hobbies…"

"I lift weights, jog, work on my dirt bikes."

"All that's work-related. Our readers want to
know what you like to do for enjoyment."

"Let's see… *Enjoyment.*" The word dripped
from his tongue with just enough intimacy to lure
her gaze to his. "I think you, of all people, should
know the answer to that one."

"How would I know…?" The question faded
as a knowing light lit her expression. "You sleep
around for enjoyment. That's what you're getting
at, isn't it?"

He grinned. "I can promise you, honey, there's
no sleeping involved." His grin widened.

Several seconds ticked by before the tension in

her muscles eased and her mouth hinted at a smile. "You're pulling my leg, aren't you?"

"I'm doing no such thing." His eyes widened in mock innocence. "I'm not even touching you." *Yet.* The unspoken promise hovered in the air between them and the temperature in the room rose another degree.

"You said yesterday that you didn't sleep around."

"I don't. You asked what I *liked* to do for enjoyment, not what I actually do."

"Which is?"

"Lift weights, jog and work on whichever bike needs it the most."

Her lips parted and her mouth curved into another smile. "You always did like to shock me."

"You were easy to shock back then. All I had to do was say a few naughty words, wink at you or look a few seconds too long, and you turned a bright shade of pink." He reached across the table before she could pull away and touched her. Not a real, hand-gripping touch. Just the slow glide of his fingertip down her forearm, to her wrist. "I've looked and winked and talked as naughty as I can with an audience around—" he motioned to Bones "—and you're still snow-white."

She met his stare. "I'm immune to your charm now that I'm all grown-up."

Another seductive slide of his finger and goose bumps rose along her arm. He smiled. "Looks like you're not so immune, after all."

"I…" She grimaced. "It's cold in here."

"You're sweating."

"I'm coming down with a cold." She pulled her

arm away from him. "You shouldn't get too close." She made a pretense of coughing. "Back to the questions."

"My thoughts exactly. Now, what about the going home alone to an empty house? You said yes and no. What did you mean?"

"Yes, I go home alone, but not to an empty house."

"Meaning?'

"I share it with twins."

"As in roommates?"

"Babies. My babies."

"You've got *kids*?"

"Barely six weeks." She grinned. "Two healthy, bouncing baby boys who just learned how to tinkle on a newspaper."

Kids. Annie had kids. Bouncing boys who tinkled on a— "Come again?"

The warmest laugh he'd ever heard vibrated from her full lips. "They're collie pups from the same litter."

Relief crept through him. "You really had me going."

"You played right into my hands."

He winked. "Right where I want to be, honey."

Her smile dissolved and she cleared her throat. "On to the last question. Your, um, fondest memory of Inspiration."

"That's easy. The homecoming game. Or rather, afterward." Tack shifted his attention to her mouth. Her full bottom lip trembled just enough to send a lightning bolt of need straight to his groin. "I was still pumped, throwing the football around on an empty field, and there you

PLAY "LUCKY 7" AND GET
THREE FREE GIFTS!

HOW TO PLAY:

1. With a coin, carefully scratch off the silver box at the right. Then check the claim chart see what we have for you — **FREE BOOKS** and a gift — **ALL YOURS! ALL FREE!**

2. Send back this card and you'll receive brand-new Harlequin Temptation® novels. The books have a cover price of $3.75 each in the U.S. and $4.25 each in Canada, but they a yours to keep absolutely free.

3. There's no catch. You're und no obligation to buy anything. W charge nothing — ZERO — your first shipment. And you do have to make any minimum numb of purchases — not even one!

4. The fact is thousands of readers enjoy receiving books by mail from the Harlequ Reader Service® months before they're available in stores. They like the convenience home delivery and they love our discount prices!

5. We hope that after receiving your free books you'll want to remain a subscriber. E the choice is yours — to continue or cancel, any time at all! So why not take us up on c invitation, with no risk of any kind. You'll be glad you did!

YOURS FREE!

PLAY LUCKY 7 FOR THIS EXCITING FREE GIFT!

THIS SURPRISE MYSTERY GIFT COULD BE YOURS FREE WHEN YOU PLAY

LUCKY 7!

PLAY THE

Just scratch off the silver box with a coin. Then check below to see the gifts you get!

I have scratched off the silver box. Please send me all the gifts for which I qualify. I understand I am under no obligation to purchase any books, as explained on the back and on the opposite page.

342 HDL CPQ9

142 HDL CPQW
(H-T-04/99)

Name: _____

PLEASE PRINT CLEARLY

Address: _____ Apt.#: _____

City: _____

State/
Prov.: _____

Postal
Zip/Code: _____

WORTH TWO FREE BOOKS PLUS
A BONUS MYSTERY GIFT!

WORTH TWO FREE BOOKS!

WORTH ONE FREE BOOK!

TRY AGAIN!

The Harlequin Reader Service® — Here's how it works:

Accepting your 2 free books and mystery gift places you under no obligation to buy anything. You may keep the books and gift and return the shipping statement marked "cancel." If you do not cancel, about a month later we'll send you 4 additional novels and bill you just $3.12 each in the U.S., or $3.57 each in Canada, plus 25¢ delivery per book and applicable taxes if any.* That's the complete price and — compared to the cover price of $3.75 in the U.S. and $4.25 in Canada — it's quite a bargain! You may cancel at any time, but if you choose to continue, every month we'll send you 4 more books, which you may either purchase at the discount price or return to us and cancel your subscription.

*Terms and prices subject to change without notice. Sales tax applicable in N.Y. Canadian residents will be charged applicable provincial taxes and GST.

were sitting on the bleachers with no particular place to go because you were the only girl in school without a date for the homecoming dance."

A soft smile played at her lips, and he knew she was remembering, too. The darkness. The moonlight. The two of them. "I didn't know how to dance."

"If I recall, you learned pretty quick."

"I hardly moved."

"Trust me. You moved just enough, sweetheart."

"How do you know? It was so dark down by the river. There wasn't even a moon out. I couldn't see a thing."

"I didn't have to see you, Annie." His voice grew husky, raw with the sudden need clawing inside him. "I felt you. Every move. Every sigh. Every beat of your heart. You know, leaving you was the one thing I regretted more than anything."

"You didn't love me."

"I came the closest to loving you as I'd ever come to loving anybody."

He watched the play of emotions on her face, the flash of longing in her eyes, the same look he'd seen down by the creek that morning, then it disappeared, snatched away by the beautiful, controlled woman sitting across from him.

"I'm not that same naive, young girl you danced with in the flatbed of your daddy's pickup." She gathered up her camera bag and notebook and started toward the back door. "And I'm not falling into bed with you again."

"Actually," he said as her gaze collided with his one last time and the fantasy that had been haunting him night after night flashed in his mind. "It wasn't a bed I had in mind."

8

TACK CLIMBED on his bike early the next morning, flipped the key and gunned the engine. A roar split open the morning silence, drowning the quiet that had haunted him all the way from the creek.

No soft footsteps or the faint *click, click* of a camera. No hushed sighs or barely contained moans. No Annie.

Starts, he told himself, determined to shift his thoughts. To focus.

He had to work on his starts.

He took a last visual survey of the makeshift track, an empty pasture covered with fresh, hard-packed dry dirt delivered just yesterday. Ruts cornered the pasture, along with several whoop sections—long rolls of dirt gutted with sharp grooves—and a few jumps. It wasn't even close to the track he trained at back in California, but it would do.

Moving his body up toward the fuel tank, he leaned over the bar and pushed his head over the front of the bike. Two fingers on the clutch, he squeezed the bike with his thighs and applied steady throttle. The motorcycle bolted forward, straight and smooth, eating up ground at a frenzied pace. Bones kept up with him for a few seconds, until Tack opened up the Kawasaki all the way.

He squared off a sharp corner the way he always did, using the rut as a traction device. *Extend your inside leg. Feed out the clutch and roll on the throttle. Easy now...* He hit the pivot point, pulled in the clutch and locked up the rear brake to get a little skid going.

Dirt flew, his body twisted and the bike gobbled up the next stretch, headed for the first whoop section up ahead.

No Annie.

It shouldn't surprise him. Hell, it didn't, not after she'd made it very clear that she wasn't sleeping with him.

But for a few days she'd come to watch him. And though he much preferred a little one-on-one, watching Annie, seeing her take her pleasure, had been as fulfilling as taking his own. Her lashes at half-mast, her lips parted, pure rapture on her sweet face. It was a sight he wasn't likely to forget for a long, long time—

The thought shattered as his front tire hit the whoop. *Wheelie in, man. Wheelie in!* But it was too late. He pulled back, the front wheel snapped up, then slapped back down and the bike jumped. Tack gripped the handlebars and fought for balance. Brakes screeched as he brought the motorcycle to a bone-jolting halt.

"Shit!" He cursed at his loss of control, his wandering thoughts. But most of all, he swore because he wanted Annie and he couldn't have her, and that realization bothered him a hell of a lot more than the fact that, for the first time in years,

Tack Brandon had lost his precious focus and nearly busted his ass.

A low whistle split the air. "I heard tell that Mr. All-Star Motocross Racer had taken up residence out here, but after witnessing that pitiful ride, I'd say I must've heard wrong."

Tack yanked off his helmet and glanced at the cowboy who stood on the other side of the fence, hat tipped back, a grin curving his familiar features.

At well over six feet, James Mission towered over most of the men in Inspiration. Except Tack.

They'd been the same height in school, always next to each other on the top row in a class picture, and side by side when it came to getting into trouble. Double Trouble, that's what everybody had called them, particularly the women. Jimmy, with his blond hair and green eyes, had been every girl's dream, and Tack, with his dark good looks and wicked charm, had been every mama's nightmare.

Tack grinned, climbed off the bike and strode toward the fence. "It's been a long time." He clasped Jimmy's hand while Bones barked his own greeting from the other side of the pasture where he'd spotted a rabbit.

"Eli said I'd find you out here. He said you were doing laps, but it looked more like that lap was doing you, buddy."

Tack shrugged at the observation. "I was just warming up."

"You'd better get a hell of a lot warmer if you intend to lead the Kawasaki team."

Tack eyed his old friend. "You follow motor-cycle racing?"

"I catch it every now and then on cable. So what's the scoop? I swear, every sportscaster from here to New York is speculating on what the hell's taking you so long to make up your mind. You racing for Kawasaki or not?"

"Hell, yes. They made a damn good offer." One he'd be a fool to pass up. So why hadn't he signed the contract? He forced the question aside and smiled. "How have you been, Jimmy?"

"Busy." The man pulled off worn brown work gloves. "Otherwise I would have come here sooner. I'm running three thousand head over at my place and there's always something to do."

"What about that little brother of yours?"

"You know Jack. Can't sit still long enough to tie his shoelaces much less look after a ranch. Last I heard, he was in New Mexico training horses for some rancher, but that won't last long. It never does with Jack. Once the newness wears off and he's met the latest challenge, he's on to something else. Someone else."

Tack chuckled. "I won't ask if he's settled down with a wife and kids."

"No kids, thankfully, but he's been married twice, and divorced three times."

Tack wiped the perspiration from his forehead. "Hell, Jimmy, I never paid much attention in Mrs. Spades's math class, but isn't the second one supposed to be less than or equal to?"

"That's what I said, but Jack never did explain that one."

"What about you?" Tack asked. "Anybody waiting at home?"

The man shook his head. "Not yet, but I've been shopping around." He winked. "Sampling the merchandise, too. How about you?"

"I'm not in the market."

"That's not what I hear." At Tack's sharp glance, Jimmy grinned. "It's a small town, Brandon."

"I thought Annie and I might get reacquainted while I'm back in town, but she's putting up one heck of a fight."

"Sounds like Annie."

"Not the one I used to know."

"You haven't been around for a long time. Annie isn't so worried about everybody liking her like when we were kids. She's got a little vinegar in her now. Like that in a woman, myself."

So did Tack. Annie had turned out to be strong and sassy and sexy as anything and he *really* liked it.

Tack's fingers clenched for a long moment, until Bones bounded up, jumping and barking, demanding a snack. He reached into his duffel bag hooked over the fence post, retrieved an orange and tossed it. The dog raced off in hot pursuit. "You seem to know an awful lot about her."

"A buyer's market. A guy's got to know the local product." At Tack's cutting look, Jimmy grinned. "Don't get yourself all worked up. She's a pretty thing, but she's not my type."

Tack raised an eyebrow. "Not enough balls?"

Jimmy frowned. "Deb Strickland gives the entire female population a bad name."

"She seemed nice enough to me."

"She's nice to everything in pants. That's half the trouble."

"And the other half is she doesn't drop her panties when you walk into the room?" At Jimmy's sharp glance, Tack chuckled. "That's it. They finally made a woman immune to Jimmy Mission's charm and it doesn't sit too well."

"Did I say it was good to see you?"

"No."

"That's because it isn't."

Tack chuckled. "You're just as glad to see me as I am you. It's been too damn long."

"And it's going to be a brief reunion if the rumor I heard is true. You really selling?"

Tack nodded and wondered why the one action bothered him so much. "I'm not cut out to cowboy."

"You made a pretty decent cowboy way back when. Remember when we used to go out chasing calves?"

Tack grinned. "I recall a few calves chasing us."

"Before we figured out how to do it right. Once we did, we put on a hell of a show. Eli said you took to the saddle again like a hog to a mud puddle."

He shrugged. "I ride bikes for a living. Same concept."

"Or maybe you're good at it, and that doesn't sit too well with you." He scratched his temple and stared off at the open pasture. "I suspect that's probably why you're selling. Afraid you might turn out to have something in common with the old man, after all."

We have nothing in common. He was a cold, manipulative bastard. A killer. The denial jumped to his tongue, and stalled there. He shook his head. "I've got a life someplace else now that has nothing to do with horses or cattle or land, and I like it that way." It was *his* life, a life he'd carved out for himself, on his own. *No ties. No debts.*

"If you're determined to let the place go, then I'd like to make a bid. Your place borders mine and the land is too good to pass up." At Tack's nod, Jimmy added, his voice somber, "I'm real sorry about Coop. If there's anything I can do, just say the word."

Tail wagging, Bones found his way back to Tack, went up on his hind legs and begged for more food.

A smile tugged at Tack's mouth as he turned to Jimmy. "You know, there is one thing…"

ANNIE EASED BACK into the trees, careful that the two men standing near the fence didn't see her.

She leaned back against a tree trunk and closed her eyes, her heart pounding frantically. So much for trying to avoid Tack. She'd purposely decided to work on land shots—some views of the pasture, the herd—all far away from the creek and, most of all, him. After their interview yesterday, the heat his hungry gaze and his charming smiles had generated, Annie wasn't about to risk seeing him again.

Not with a peach in his hand and sin on his mind.

She wanted only to finish her job. The sooner she finished the pictures, the sooner the sales package could be put together and a buyer found. The sooner Tack Brandon would leave Inspiration.

She peered around the tree, her heart jumping into her throat as she drank in the sight of him. He wore only a sleeveless black racing vest with Take the Dare emblazoned in liquid blue. Matching black pants hugged his thighs and calves. Biker boots completed the outfit. His hair was damp. Perspiration dripped off his chin. Bare muscular arms gleamed with sweat. He looked tired and hot and...incredibly sexy.

Her pulse quickened and heat uncurled low in her belly, spiraling to the sensitive tips of her breasts. She became acutely aware of the way her lacy bra rasped against her nipples with every deep breath.

Distance, she told herself. *Turn around and don't look back.*

Surprisingly, her body obeyed. Fifteen minutes later, she climbed into her truck parked on the side of the dirt road that bordered the wildflower field, *her* field, and tried the key. The engine refused to catch.

"Please don't do this to me now." She tried again.

Click, click, click...

She slammed her palm against the steering wheel and let loose Deb's favorite four-letter expletive. "First the stupid air conditioner at home, and now this. Why me?"

She wallowed in self-pity all of five seconds before she climbed out, popped the hood and tried to figure out what she was looking for. She checked the oil, the water in the radiator and tapped and knocked a few places. Another turn of the key and still nothing.

So much for speeding up Tack's departure. If she didn't get the film to the lab before noon, she would never have the pictures by five. That meant waiting until Monday. Three extra days.

Annie grabbed her camera equipment and started walking.

A few minutes down the road, the roar of a motorcycle filled her ears and she moved to the shoulder just as a familiar black Harley grumbled to a stop beside her. Tack sat there, hands on his hips, blue eyes roaming from her head to her dust-covered sandals.

"My truck quit," she explained.

"I saw it a ways back. Could be the transmission. It was leaking fluid."

She shook her head. "Just my luck."

He grinned. "You could get lucky in a second, honey, if you wanted to." There was no missing the double meaning.

"I'm not interested in getting lucky."

His unreadable blue eyes assessed her. "Or maybe you're just afraid."

"Of you?" Her laugh sounded rusty.

"Of finding out that you're a hell of a lot more affected by me than you care to admit."

He couldn't have been more wrong. Annie already knew the truth, felt it in the bone-melting heat that gripped her body, the electricity that skimmed her nerve endings when he was near.

She tried for a laugh. "That'll be the day."

"Then get on." His eyes gleamed with challenge and Annie knew she had no choice. She either climbed on or walked, and walking would be as good as admitting that Tack Brandon did, indeed, get to her.

"I only need to go as far as Moby's Service Station. He's got a wrecker." She straddled the spot behind him and gripped the sides of the seat, careful to avoid touching him.

As if he sensed her reluctance, he said, "You'd better hold on to me unless you want to find yourself lying by the side of the road." He chuckled, a soft, warm, sexy sound that vibrated the air around them. "I won't bite, honey. Unless you want me to, that is."

"No, thanks." She took a deep breath, braced herself and slid her arms around his waist. "Okay, I'm ready."

And so was he, she realized when he shifted the bike into gear and zoomed forward. They jumped and Annie's hands grazed the bulge in his jeans.

She stiffened and he chuckled again. "The service station?" he asked. "You sure that's as far as you want to go, honey? Because I could take you for a long ride." The deep huskiness of his voice told her the ride he referred to had nothing to do with motorcycles and everything to do with a man and woman and lots of sweet, breathstealing bumps and curves. "Long and slow. Short and fast. Any way you want it."

She wasn't going to let him bait her. "Moby's is plenty far enough."

But Tack had other ideas. He took her to Moby's and helped make the necessary arrangements to have her truck picked up. Then he steered her back onto the Harley, determined to see her safely to work.

By the time Annie climbed off the back of Tack's motorcycle, she was this close to throwing herself across the front of his bike and begging him to touch her, kiss her, love her.

Close, but not quite there. *Yet.*

"Don't I get a thank-you?"

"Thank you," she said, grabbing her camera bag.

"I was thinking of something a little more... *active.*" He grinned, oblivious to Mr. Hopkins and several others who stood out in front of a nearby grocery store, their gazes hooked on Tack and Annie. "Like a kiss."

"Didn't you hear anything I said?"

"That you're not falling into bed with me again. I don't see a bed around, honey. It's just a kiss."

"Forget it." She glanced pointedly at Mr. Hopkins.

"Afraid people might get the wrong idea about us?"

Or the right idea. "I'm not kissing you, and I don't give a fig what anyone thinks."

"Well, then." He climbed off the motorcycle to tower in front of her. "I guess I'll have to kiss you."

Before she could blink, he hauled her up against his chest and covered her lips with his. His tongue slid into her mouth to stroke and tease. Strong hands pressed the small of her back, holding her close as he kissed her long and slow and deep the way he had in the newspaper office Saturday night. But this time she could feel every inch of his body, from chest to hips to thighs, his desire pressing hard and eager into her belly.

He smelled of leather and fresh air and a touch of wildness that teased her nostrils and made her breathe heavier, desperate to draw more of his essence into her lungs.

She was a heartbeat away from sliding her arms around his neck and clinging to him, when she heard the high-pitched whistle followed by a few shouts of encouragement from their audience.

Annie did what any woman would have done in her situation. She grabbed an inch of Tack's upper arm and pinched for all she was worth.

"Ouch!" He released her with a suddenness that sent her stumbling backward a few steps. "What the hell was that for?"

"For kissing me when I didn't want a kiss."

He rubbed his arm. "You could have tried telling me to stop before you decided to take off an inch of flesh."

"You weren't giving me much room to get a word in edgewise."

He examined his arm. "Hell, it's bruising."

"It was only a little pinch."

"I think you broke the skin," he said accusingly.

"I did not." She leaned in and rubbed a fingertip over the spot of angry red skin. "Don't be such a baby." She summoned her courage and ignored a pang of guilt. "And don't kiss me again. Otherwise, I just might break the skin."

Despite his bruised arm, he chuckled. "You know, honey," he said, his eyes darkening to a deep sapphire blue, "I might be inclined to think you don't like me, except that you were really into that kiss."

She bristled. "In your dreams, buddy. I pinched you, remember?"

"*Before* you pinched me. You kissed me back, Annie. Both lips, tongue, the works, baby. *You* kissed *me*." With a satisfied smile, he turned, climbed on the motorcycle and left her staring after him.

She wasn't sure how she made it across the sidewalk and up the stairs to the newspaper office. Divine intervention. Or maybe the fact that she could feel the eyes on her, boring into her back after Tack's blatant disregard for their rapt audience.

He'd kissed her on Main Street in front of God and everyone.

It doesn't matter what people think.

Ordinarily, but this wasn't some misconception based on ignorance. Anyone who saw the kiss would know that Tack Brandon wanted Annie Divine.

At least they didn't know that she wanted him back. She'd pinched him and put him in his place. If only she'd done it a moment sooner. Before she'd kissed him back with both lips, tongue, the works.

Her stomach jumped as she walked into the office and sat down to find a stack of mail on her desk. A quick thumb through the pile and her day went from bad to worse. Five rejection letters from the five résumés she'd sent out, and all in one week.

"It's a tough business." Deb walked by, her Bad To The Bitchiest Bone mug in her hand, sympathy gleaming in her eyes. "Don't let it get to you. Send out more tear sheets."

Annie nodded, filed the letters away in her drawer and pulled out her Top Twenty list. She crossed off the rejections and moved on to the next batch of five.

They were just a few rejections, a few stop signs on the road to her future, and it was just one kiss.

Okay, so technically it was two, but that didn't matter as long as the buck stopped here.

No more kissing. Nada. Zilch.

If only she didn't want to go for number three.

Annie wasn't taking any chances on another encounter with Tack. She dropped the ranch pictures by Gary Tucker's office at exactly 5:00 p.m., stopped off at the garage to check on her truck, then headed back to the office to finish some work.

She sat down at her desk and pulled out another manila envelope. The pictures she hadn't turned over to Gary.

She stared down at a particularly suggestive shot of Tack eating a peach down by the creek.

Now was her chance. Deb was still at the courthouse interviewing the mayor's secretary for a political piece. Wally was downstairs with the printing press that kept eating this week's issue.

Out of sight, out of mind.

She gripped the edge of one and started to tear. Her fingers faltered a fraction from his face. He wore such an intense expression, as if he put all his heart and soul into the simple task of devouring the fruit, sating his hunger, stirring hers. A smile tugged at her lips, and she tucked the photos into her camera bag.

What harm could a few mementos do?

"DID YOU get pictures?" Deb stood in front of Annie's desk less than an hour later, a copy of Tack's interview in one hand and her Born To Bitch mug in the other.

"Pictures?" Annie's squeaked out, shifting a guilty gaze to her camera bag. "What pictures?"

"Of Tack. A head and neck shot for the This Is Your Neighbor column. We usually run the article with at least one picture."

"Oh, *that* picture."

"What else?"

"Nothing." Annie tried to still her pounding heart as she rummaged in her desk and pulled out the yearbook she'd used to fill in background information on Tack. "How about this?"

"An old yearbook photograph?"

"That's how the entire town remembers him. We can use a few football shots, the standard head and shoulders. It'll be like a tribute to the past." And the only thing Annie could come up with since she'd been so worked up during the interview, she'd forgotten to take a current picture.

"How about this prom photo?" Deb wiggled her eyebrows. "Geez, honey, you were a pretty girl, but that is the ugliest dress I've ever seen. All

I see is a little blond head sitting on top of this navy blue...*thing*."

"I wasn't a flashy dresser back then."

"And you landed the captain of the football team?"

"I think that was one of the reasons Tack liked me. I wasn't flashing my cleavage in his face every five minutes. He liked the challenge."

"This was definitely a challenge. I'd say the guy deserves a date just for the effort."

"I do not have any desire to date Tack Brandon. He's only back for a little while." Thankfully. "And I'm busy."

"Doing what? Your weekly stories are finished. We go to press in the morning. It's Friday night and you're free."

"Not completely. I already have a date."

"With who?"

"My living room. I'm wallpapering tonight. Ivory with mauve flowers," Annie said. "And it's gorgeous."

"Not half as gorgeous as this." Deb pointed to the photo of Tack.

But much safer, she thought as she headed across the street to Heavenly Hardware to pick up the wallpaper supplies and the paste before she hitched a ride home with Deb.

And safe was all Annie could handle right now.

9

LATER THAT EVENING, Annie stood on a stepladder, struggled with a strip of wallpaper and tried not to think about Tack.

Or his kiss.

Or that she wanted, *really* wanted another.

Work. She steeled herself and tried to concentrate on the paste-laden strip of wallpaper rather than the restless hunger gnawing at her, the need to feel his lips on hers, his hands skimming her body, his heart beating strong and sure and frantic against hers—

The screen door shook with the force of a knock, shattering her thoughts. Thankfully.

"Come on in," she called out over the radio blasting an old Rolling Stones song. The wallpaper sagged with the weight of the paste and she struggled to hold the sheet upright. "They ought to give a warning with this stuff. Extra hands needed." She groaned as the edges started to fold over. The screen door squeaked and she added, "That was quick. Just put the pizza on the table."

"What pizza?"

The deep voice froze her hand in midair. The paper collapsed, slapping her cheek as she realized that Tack Brandon stood in her living room.

Worse, he was standing right behind her. He

leaned in, strong, muscular arms coming up on either side to help her hold up the paper.

His large, dark hands were a stark contrast against the dainty cream wallpaper as he anchored the edges in place. Annie managed to tear her attention away from the tanned perfection of his fingers long enough to retrieve the wallpaper blade from her pocket and smooth the strip into place. Her fingers trembled. Her heart drummed. Or maybe that was his. He was so close. Too close.

"I—I thought you were the pizza boy."

"Not the last time I looked."

His voice rumbled over her bare shoulder. Warm breath brushed her skin, sending a wave of goose bumps chasing down the length of her arm. She managed a few more swipes of the blade then slipped it back into her pocket.

"All done," she said, but he didn't move. Annie turned in his arms. The stepladder put her at eye level with him and their gazes collided. Locked.

"It looks good," he said, but his eyes remained on her.

"I—I always thought wallpaper would look nice in here."

"I wasn't talking about the wallpaper."

Suddenly, she couldn't get enough air. She drew in a deep breath, the motion pushing her breasts up and out. Her nipples kissed his chest. Heat spiraled from the points of contact to settle low in her belly.

"What are you doing here?" she managed to say in a breathy voice.

What would you like me to do? That's what his

gaze said, but his lips murmured, "You said you were fixing up the place." He spared the chaos around them a quick glance, from the sheet-covered furniture and scarred hardwood floor, to the torn screen door. Bones stood on the other side, wet nose pressed to the mesh, while the twins barked and jumped at him from the inside. Tack's gaze returned to hers and a slow grin spread across his face. "I thought I could help. I'm pretty good with my hands."

Too good. The thought blew through her mind a second before he touched her. A callused finger-tip slid along her sweaty cheek, the damp skin of her neck.

Electricity skimmed her nerve endings, sending warmth pulsing to her nipples, her thighs.

"You're awful hot, honey."

She blew out a breath. "My air conditioner conked out. The hardware store special-ordered a part, but it's not in yet."

He didn't seem convinced. He stared at her as if searching for answers. Despite the radio blasting in the background and the twins yipping and yapping at Bones, she could hear the air drawing in and out of her lungs, the drumming of her own heart, the hum of blood as it zipped through her veins.

"That explains why you're so wet." His gaze dropped, roaming over her neck and shoulders covered with a fine sheen of sweat, down over the damp material of her tank top molded to her puckered nipples, the bare skin of her stomach glistening just above the waistband of her shorts.

Blue eyes caught and held hers. "That *is* why you're so wet, isn't it?"

Before she could answer, the twins abandoned Bones and rushed at Tack, effectively breaking the erotic spell holding Annie captive.

"I—I'm going to open another window." She didn't look at him as she ducked beneath one arm and stepped off the ladder, but she felt his grin.

"Hey, there, fellas." Tack hefted the twins into his arms. They licked at his face, tails wagging. "Gary said the pictures were really good."

"Thanks."

"He's handling the Echo Canyon sale in the next county and asked if you'd be interested in earning some extra cash. He said to give him a call." He nuzzled the puppies. "You cheated, you know," he finally said. "You were supposed to deliver the pictures to me."

She averted her gaze and fought to push the living-room windows as high as they would go. "Gary's in charge of the sale, so I thought I'd give them directly to him and save some time."

"Or maybe you weren't in any big hurry to see me again."

"Maybe I wasn't."

"Why not?"

She gave an indifferent shrug. "Why should I be?"

He stared at her as if searching for an answer, and she feared he wasn't going to let the subject go. Then a grin slid across his handsome face and relief crept through her.

"Because I'm cute," he offered.

"More like egotistical."

"Irresistible," he countered.

"Shameless."

"Helpful. You need an extra pair of hands, and here I am."

Speaking of hands...

Her gaze fixed on his, so big and strong and tanned and gentle against the small white puppies. *Gentle.* A warmth spread through her, soothing her jangled nerves. "I guess I could use the help." She wiped at the sweat beading her forehead. "I'll paste and you do the hanging."

"I'm way ahead of you on that, honey."

A quick glance down and she realized he wasn't speaking just figuratively. She blushed, he chuckled, and despite the sexual tension coiling around them, she actually relaxed.

She liked his laugh. The deep sound of his voice. The teasing. He could always make her feel at ease even though she knew he posed the greatest threat. Because Tack Brandon had been her friend, as well as her lover. Her best friend, and for some insane reason, that's all she remembered at the moment.

They spent the next half hour finishing one wall until the real pizza boy arrived. While Tack moved the sofa to the opposite side of the room so they could paper the next wall, Annie let the twins out to do their business. When she returned, she found him sitting on the floor with her pink photo album.

"It fell off the coffee table during the move," he explained as he turned page after page, his gaze drinking in everything from photos to a cocktail napkin from her mother's favorite restaurant, a dried daisy—her mother's favorite flower. "What is it?" he said, indicating the album.

"My mom."

He closed the book as his gaze locked with hers. "You mean it belonged to her?"

"I mean it *is* her. It's filled with everything she loved in her life. Whenever I get lonely, I look at it and it makes me feel closer to her." She held out her hand. "I'll put it away so it doesn't get messed up."

"That's nice," he finally said as he handed over the album, and Annie realized she'd been holding her breath. A strange sense of relief stole through her and she smiled.

She stored the album under her bed, retrieved two beers and some napkins from the kitchen, then joined Tack in the living room. She handed him a bottle dripping with condensation.

"I've never developed a taste for the stuff myself—this is Deb's leftover from our last gab session—but it's the only thing that's really cold in this entire house." She sank onto the floor and sat with her legs crossed, the pizza separating them.

He took a long swig of beer and glanced around.

Annie's gaze followed his, from the leak in the ceiling where water had puckered the sheetrock, to the scratched floor, to the broken screen door. "I was so busy making ends meet after my mom died that I let the place go. I mean, it never was much, but my mom kept up with everything. Minor repairs, fresh paint, waxed floors. Since I never had a dad, except biologically speaking, she learned how to fend for herself."

"Do you remember him at all?"

"Only what she told me. He was a truck driver. She'd just graduated high school and started waitressing at this honky-tonk out on the interstate. They were both young and in lust. She told him when she found out she was pregnant, and never saw him again after that. He left town. She had me and moved us here, as far away as her pocketbook and a Greyhound bus could carry us. She promised that Inspiration would only be temporary, just long enough for her to save some money and get us to Austin."

"What was in Austin?"

"The Silver Spurs, the biggest nightclub in Texas, or it was at the time. They had their own version of the Rockettes who wore these little cowgirl outfits and put on nightly shows."

"She wanted to be a dancer?"

"A respectable dancer. A showgirl. But she never made it."

"Because she met my father."

"And fell in love, and gave up her dreams, to stay here and be the town outcast." A mistake Annie had no intention of repeating. Her dreams had seen her through the pain of Tack's leaving and given her hope for something other than him riding back into town and sweeping her off her feet like the hero in some romantic fairy tale. "Not me."

"Which part?"

"All three. I've spent my entire life living for everyone else. Now I want something for myself. I want to take my career as far as it can go."

"I guess that means you haven't given much thought to settling down."

She shrugged. "Ted Riley asks me to dinner every once in a while. He's the youth minister over at the church. We've kissed a few times, but nothing more. We're mainly just friends." She watched a satisfied expression creep over Tack's face. "What about you? You ever think about tying the knot?"

He took another swig of beer and wiped his sweaty forehead. "No, and I intend to keep it that way. I'm not the marrying kind. I'm on the road a lot, living out of a suitcase. My racing takes one hundred and ten percent. That's no kind of life for a wife and kids." He paused, then said, "I'm not making the same mistake as my old man. He was too busy with his ranch to do right by my mother and me."

"Sounds awful cynical for the guy voted most likely to."

"To what?"

She grinned. "Just *to*. The Tack Brandon I knew would try anything at least once."

"And the Annie Divine I knew wanted a big white wedding and at least three kids."

Before Annie could think of a reply, Bones whimpered from the front porch. Annie got to her feet and let him in, grateful for the sudden distraction. He rushed over to Tack and begged for some pizza.

After the dog had devoured his fourth slice, Annie asked, "Does he always eat this much?"

"You wouldn't think so from looking at him. But he's a glutton, aren't you, boy?" He rubbed the dog's head and Bones wagged his tail. "I've been trying to find him a home, but so far he's been to three different places and has eaten himself right into a trip back to the Big B. He was with Jimmy until yesterday. Bones ate Jimmy's lunch, then left a little souvenir in Jimmy's boot."

"You don't mean—"

"Jimmy's still trying to get the smell out." Tack climbed to his feet, grabbed the empty pizza box and the napkins and stuffed them into a nearby trash bag Annie had erected for the wallpaper leftovers.

"He's kind of cute." Annie rubbed the dog's bulging tummy. "And he probably pooped in Jimmy's boot because he was lonesome for you. Dogs do that when they're homesick."

"The Big B isn't his home." Tack lowered himself to the floor, his back against the wall, his legs stretched out in front of him. "Damn, but it's hot in here." He pulled at his damp T-shirt and Annie caught a glimpse of a rock-hard abdomen dusted with dark hair.

She forced her attention back to Bones. "I meant, he probably missed you. Why don't you keep him?"

"I don't think he'd fit in my suitcase. I'm on the road two-thirds of the year, and I'm hardly home when I *am* home. I can't keep him."

Bones rolled over to waddle around Tack, and settle down beside him.

Annie laughed. "You might not be keeping him, but I think he wants to keep you."

"Actually, it's your floor he's getting real comfortable on. Help a guy out, Annie. Bones here would be in heaven. Animals like you."

"If memory serves me, they like you, too. I seem to recall a certain collie that followed you everywhere."

He grinned. "Mary Theresa."

"Who ever heard of calling a dog Mary Theresa?"

"Nostalgia, honey. Mary Theresa was the first female I ever had a crush on. My kindergarten teacher. Mary Theresa Berger. What about you? Name your first love."

"That's easy. Pastor Marley." At his incredulous expression, she shrugged. "What can I say? I liked the way he looked in that suit." She took a sip of beer. "I remember sitting in the last pew—I always sat in the last one because I had to ride the Sunday-school bus and, since I lived so far out, I was always getting there late. Anyhow, I would slide into my seat and sit there and think, if I could just marry Reverend Marley, my life would be perfect."

"Wasn't he bald?"

"And he wore glasses and had a potbelly, but it wasn't about looks."

"What was it about?"

Annie stiffened and shook her head. "I think we've strolled down memory lane enough for one night. This wallpaper won't hang itself." She started to climb to her feet. Large, strong fingers closed around hers.

"Come on, Annie. Tell me."

She wasn't sure why she did, except that he was touching her and she did crazy things when he touched her. "I thought that if I married Pastor Marley, I'd get to sit in the front row for once. People would shake my hand and smile at me instead of staring at me, or worse, pretending not to see me at all."

"I see you," he said, his thumb rubbing a tiny circle at the inside of her wrist. "I always did." He let go of her then, but it was too late. Her nipples tightened, tingled, and a low burning flame swept her nerve endings, and all because of that small, whisper-soft touch that had lasted all of two seconds.

She let out an unsteady breath. "It's really hot in here."

"I know the feeling." He drank the last of his beer and set the bottle down. Bones shifted and stepped over Tack. The bottle *clinked* to its side as the dog strolled toward the kitchen.

Tack eyed the fallen beer bottle, then a slow grin spread across his face. With a flick of his wrist, he started the bottle spinning. It shimmied to a standstill, the mouth pointing to Annie.

His eyes gleamed with challenge. "Truth or dare?"

Maybe it was the heat or the beer or his smile, maybe all three, that reminded her of so many hot nights sitting by the river, spinning a cola bottle in the back of his daddy's truck and playing kissing games. Regardless, she met his gaze, his smile, and whispered, "Truth."

"Did you miss me?"

She swallowed, thought about lying, then quickly discarded it. "You were one of my best friends. Of course I missed you."

"That's not the kind of miss I meant." He grinned. "But it'll do. For now. Your turn."

Annie's fingers trembled as she twirled the bottle, which came to point at her again. "I think this is rigged."

"Truth or dare?"

"Another spin?"

"That's against the rules." He eyed her. "But just to show you that I'm a nice guy, I'll give you another chance."

Annie smiled and twirled the bottle again. "Aha," she said, smiling triumphantly. "Truth or dare?"

"Truth."

"Did *you* miss *me*?"

"You were my best friend..." He started to mimic her answer and disappointment welled inside. "And my lover, and I missed both. You've been keeping me company at night, Annie." Fierce blue eyes caught and held hers. "In my dreams. But they've been even worse lately since I've been back in town." He paused, his voice dropping to a husky whisper, "And back inside of you—"

"Your turn," she blurted before he could say any more. "Your spin." She pushed the bottle at him. "Here. Spin."

He did. The bottle pointed to her. "Truth or dare?" he asked.

Annie wasn't up to any more questions. "Dare."

He didn't say anything for a long moment, just stared at her, his gaze dark, intense, stirring.

"Kiss me like you missed me," he finally said. "Like you *really* missed me."

Pleasure tickled low in her belly at the prospect, and before she could call it quits, she got to her knees and scooted closer. It was just a kiss, one she wanted more than her next breath.

She focused on that thought, rather than the push-pull of emotion inside her, and placed her hands on his broad shoulders to steady herself.

"No pinching this time," he added, his warm breath feathering her lips.

She smiled. "And here I thought this was going to be fun."

"Oh, it'll be fun, all right. Just not life-threatening."

"Says you," she murmured as she touched her mouth to his.

One kiss, Tack told himself as she leaned in, one simple kiss. That's all she owed him, all he meant to collect.

Until her lips lingered, parted and a soft moan quivered into his mouth, and suddenly he wanted more than a kiss.

Suddenly he wanted more than teasing games. He wanted to make his dreams come true. To feel her pulse around him and shatter in his arms. To feel *her*, warm and quivering and real.

His hands came up, sliding around her waist and pulling her closer. One hand caught the back of her thigh, lifting her knee so that she straddled him. He grabbed her bottom and settled her more firmly against the bulge in his jeans.

The contact shocked them both. She gasped and rocked against him, and he worked frantically at the button of her shorts. The zipper hissed, the waistband fell open and his fingers dived inside. He cupped the soft flesh of her buttocks in his bare hands.

The heat burned fierce between them as they kissed and rubbed and worked each other into a frenzy. The air grew hotter, charged with the summer heat and the ripe smell of sweaty bodies and steamy sex and—

"Wait." His fingers tightened, stilling her movements. "Slow down, honey. I don't want this to go too fast, to be over too quick." He took a deep breath and rested his forehead against hers. "Damn, you make me crazy. I can't think."

"It's the beer," she murmured before claiming his lips in another kiss.

Another sweet, erotic shimmy of her body and the air lodged in his chest.

"I can't breathe either," he gasped.

"It's the heat."

Beer? Heat? He caught her face between his hands. Her gaze collided with his. "Like hell, Annie. It's you. Me. *Us*."

Denial raged in her eyes, warring with the passion that glittered hot and bright and needy.

He was so close to easing the fierce ache. A quick flick of a button, a swift jerk on his zipper and he could satisfy them both.

But for the first time in his life, Tack wanted more from a woman than physical satisfaction. He wanted to know why. Why the tears, the murmured, "It's been so long." *Why?*

"You do this to me," he said, arching so she felt every thick, throbbing inch of him through his jeans. "And I do this to you." He flicked her puckered nipple, making it quiver and tighten, before trailing his fingers down to dip into her shorts, her panties and stroke the moist heat between her legs. "I make you this hot, this wet."

"I haven't been with anyone in a while and—" she caught her bottom lip as his fingertip dipped inside her "—I...I'm only human. It's so hot in here and I have needs and..." The sentence faded into a whimper.

"Needs that could be satisfied by any man?"

"Y-yes."

He plunged deep and she shuddered. Her eyes closed, her full lips parted. He indulged her for two more deep, probing thrusts before stilling the movements, for his own sanity more than hers. She was so damn beautiful, so flushed and hot and ready, and he was only human. Only a man. *Her* man.

"You know, honey," he said when her eyes fluttered open. "I'm not nearly as convinced that what happened between us my first night back in town, that this—" another sweet probe of his finger and a ragged gasp broke from her full lips "—is just for convenience's sake, that you're hungry for a man and I happen to fit that description. There's more to it. More than the beer freeing your inhibitions or the heat making your body burn."

"There isn't," she said, despite the fact that she arched into him, her muscles contracting, drawing him a fraction deeper.

Ah...

He couldn't help himself. He kissed her, a

deep, probing kiss that uncovered every secret and left no doubt in her mind that he wanted her.

"Just to prove my point," he murmured when the kiss ended and he finally found his voice, "I'm not going to press you, or touch you or kiss you again or—" he licked his lips in slow, sensuous promise "—do half the things running through my mind. Not until you say the word, until you ask me. That way, if you're not attracted to *me*, then you don't have a thing to worry about. I won't tempt you, and there'll be no fall from grace." He gathered his last shred of control, removed his hand from her shorts and felt her tremble at the slide of flesh along flesh.

She was hiding. Hiding her need for him behind convenient excuses that could explain her reaction in purely physical terms.

But this was more than physical. The chemistry between them was explosive because the feelings ran deeper than lust. Much deeper.

He fastened her shorts, set her aside and climbed to his feet. Then he walked away from her, because Tack Brandon wanted more than sex. For the first time in his life, he wanted a woman's heart, as well. He wanted Annie's.

ANNIE STOOD on her back porch, her body still hot and trembling, an undeniable reminder that Tack Brandon had roared back into her life, into her head and her heart.

Not for long, she told herself. He would be leaving again, and Annie would get on with her life, with her future, and she would forget all about the way his eyes darkened to a midnight blue when he looked at her. The way his hands trailed over her body, soft and tender, yet purposeful at the same time, the way he looked at her, into her, and saw all the things she tried to hide. Her desire. Her love.

Not love. Not completely. Not yet.

Out of sight, out of mind.

She opened the trash can, threw the photos inside and slammed the lid back on. Then she turned on her heel and marched inside.

She tossed and turned for the next few hours, trying to fall asleep. Just when she started to relax, she saw him standing down by the creek, eating the peach with enough zest to make her legs quiver. She felt him, too. His hands on her breasts, feathering over her skin, stroking between her legs until she was so close to coming apart—

She threw off the covers, hurried outside and retrieved the photos from the trash can.

"This doesn't prove a thing except that I hate to waste really good work." The pictures of Tack had been some of her best. They told their own story of passion and hunger, and while she wasn't about to add them to her portfolio, neither could she discard them.

She packed the pictures away in her picture box and stuffed it beneath the bed. *Safe.*

But Annie herself was far from safe. The night stretched ahead of her, the bed loomed big and empty, and Tack waited just the other side of sleep. To touch and tantalize and try to shake her precious control.

Tonight proved her point exactly. She had to

keep her distance from him until he left. In the meantime, no touching, no kissing, *nothing*.

"MISS ANNIE?" Annie turned from painting the trim at the far corner of the house, to see Wayne Mitchell, the clerk from the hardware store.

"Did I forget something?" She glanced around at the gallons of paint, the brushes and rollers, the pan.

"No. You picked up everything yesterday. I've got a temporary air-conditioning unit that Mr. Heaven asked me to bring out here and hook up until the part comes in for yours."

"I didn't ask for a temporary unit."

Wayne shrugged. "All's I know is Mr. Heaven got a call from Mr. Brandon, and here I am." He motioned to the truck. "I'll get the unit hooked up for you."

"Forget it. I'll wait for the part."

"But—"

"Take it back."

"Mr. Heaven will be mad 'cause Mr. Brandon's sure to be hot as a concrete pavement at noon if his orders ain't carried out."

"I'll take care of Mr. Brandon," she said through tight lips. "You can bet money on that."

Later, after she conned Wally into a ride, she found Tack in the barn at the Big B.

"I don't need you flaunting your money and renting air conditioners for me."

He finished saddling the horse and faced her. "I just wanted to make sure there wasn't anything clouding your opinion of what's going on between us."

"There's nothing going on between us."

"Did they get the unit hooked up?"

"I sent it back. If I want a temporary unit, I can rent one myself. I don't need anyone paying for me." *Buying* me. The way Coop had tried to buy her mother. He'd given her so many things to con her into staying, into needing him so much she'd given up her dreams of Austin so she could stay and be his mistress.

She slapped him in the chest with an envelope. "Here's the money you gave Mr. Heaven." She turned and stormed out. He caught her at the doorway, his hand closing around hers for a split second before he let her go.

"I wasn't paying for you, Annie, or trying to insult you. I was just trying to even up the playing field."

"There's no need, because we're not playing. Last night was a tie. End of season." Annie walked away, and Tack's voice followed her out.

"I've got news for you, honey. We're going into overtime."

10

IT WAS late Saturday afternoon when Tack showed up on Annie's doorstep. Freshly showered and shaved, he looked heartbreakingly handsome in a white T-shirt and jeans. When he handed her a single daisy, her chest tightened.

"I thought you might want some company. My company."

She took the flower and summoned her indifference. "What would make you think something like that?"

"You don't have to be scared, Annie."

"Of you?"

"Of us."

"There is no us. I—I really have to go." It took everything she had to close the door in his face, but she managed.

She waited for the sound of footsteps, the roar of his motorcycle. She heard only the *bam, bam, bam* of her own heart.

He wasn't leaving. The knowledge hit her a few seconds later. She moved to the edge of the curtain in time to see him shrug out of his shirt, pick up a nearby can of paint and a brush and disappear around the side of the house. Annie rushed to the back bedroom and peered through the window, and saw Tack start on the trim she'd begun that morning.

As if he had nothing better to do than help her out. As if he enjoyed it.

Fat chance. It was a ploy to get into her house, her bed.

Annie promised herself to ignore him and concentrate on varnishing the newly stripped kitchen cabinets, but it wasn't easy. She heard every sound, from the swish-swish of paint near the kitchen window as he finished the side of the house, to the glug-glug of water when he finally rinsed up and called it quits just after sunset. His Harley growled and spewed gravel as he left her to a sleepless night filled with erotic dreams of a half-naked man who smiled and teased and ate peaches and made Annie feel both shy and wanton at the same time.

That was his plan, she told herself the next day. That and to make her feel guilty that he was outside working so hard on a Sunday afternoon while she sat inside with a cool glass of lemonade.

From the sofa where she sat, she could see him through the front window that overlooked the porch. He'd finally worked his way around and had just started to apply a fresh coat to the wooden railing that framed the porch.

He wore nothing but a pair of faded jeans and dusty black motorcycle boots. The denim hung low on his hips. His muscled torso gleamed with perspiration. She shook her head at the ache that twisted her middle. Longing. Anticipation.

She stomped to the window and yanked the

blinds closed. There. That was better. She could enjoy her lemonade with no distractions—

Bones barked, shattering the thought. Annie peeked through the slats to see the dog sitting under a nearby tree, panting. Her gaze shifted back to Tack.

Strong fingers clasped the paintbrush. Muscles rippled, bulged as he moved the brush back and forth. Annie forced her attention from the slow, smooth strokes, up, over a heavily muscled bicep, the curve of one broad shoulder, to his face. Sweat beaded his forehead. A drop slid from his temple, down to his strong jaw and dropped onto his chest.

Perspiration trickled from her own temple.

Maybe she should have forked over the money herself for a temporary air-conditioning unit. Then she wouldn't be so miserable. Not that it would have offered Tack any relief. He was outside, in the one hundred and ten-plus, record-breaking heat.

Seconds later, she opened the front door, thrust a glass of lemonade at him and placed a bowl of fresh water on the front steps for Bones. Then she picked up a brush.

"What are you doing?"

"Painting. If you think I'm letting you have all the fun while I bake in that oven of a house, you've got another think coming."

It *was* just painting. Harmless, innocent painting in full view of God and Mrs. Pope and anybody else who might wander by.

Tack grinned. "I knew you couldn't resist my charm."

But it wasn't his charm she was worried about resisting. It was all the rest of him.

"WALLY HAD a dental appointment, so I told him I'd come by and give you a lift." Deb climbed out of her fire-engine-red Miata just as Annie stepped up onto the porch after giving her roses their Monday-morning watering.

"Thanks. My truck should be fixed later this afternoon."

Deb glanced around and let out a low whistle. "Wow. This place is really shaping up. I thought you'd planned to work on the inside this weekend."

"It wasn't her," came the gravelly voice next door. "It was that man, Coop Brandon's boy. He spent the whole danged weekend over there, traipsing around half-naked."

"Half-naked?" A smile split Deb's face. "Sounds interesting."

"Dreadful, that's what it was," the woman said. "If you youngsters want to play sex games, you should do it in the privacy of your own home."

"Good morning to you, too, Mrs. Pope," Annie greeted in her cheeriest voice. "Play bingo this weekend?" The woman frowned.

"Sex games." Deb's smile widened. "And here I thought I was the only one who kicked up her heels on the weekend."

"We did not play sex games," Annie told Deb. "We were just painting and drinking lemonade together."

"It was a shameful display," Mrs. Pope chimed in.

Deb motioned next door. "I thought she wore a hearing aid."

"I've never worn any such thing, missy," Mrs. Pope grumbled, stabbing the air in Deb's direction with her gardening tool. "My hearing's one hundred percent just like the rest of me. A rest home, my daughter Claire says. Why, she can shove her rest home where the sun don't shine..."

"I bet the rest home has weekly bingo," Annie called out as she grabbed Deb's arm and ushered her inside. "I swear, the woman's got bionic hearing, and the eyesight to go with it."

"At least you only have to worry about one neighbor since you live out here in the boonies." Deb poised on the edge of Annie's couch, an eager look on her face while Annie searched for her camera bag. "So tell me, are we talking so-so, it's-not-so-bad-but-I-live-in-redneck-central shameful, or the ultra, even-try-anything-once-Deb-will-be-shocked shameful."

"Neither." Annie found her bag, then hustled the twins onto the fenced-in back porch and closed the door. "Nothing happened."

"He was here."

"Yes."

"And he did all that work outside."

"Yes."

"And you were both traipsing around naked."

"That's *half*-naked, and it was Tack who took off his shirt. I was fully clothed." With the exception of Friday night, she added silently.

"So he was here strictly in a home-repair

sense." At Annie's nod, she added, "The guy's either stupid, or he wants you bad. I vote for the second. Either way, you should thank him."

"I did. I said thanks, kept him supplied with lemonade and even painted a little myself. Now, can we just go?"

Deb nodded and five minutes later they were zooming down the main strip through town.

"I don't understand why you're trying so hard to push this guy away," her friend said as she struggled to parallel park in a spot no sane person would try for, except Deb, who prided herself on her skill behind the wheel.

"You're cutting it awful close to that black Bronco behind us."

"Black?" Deb's head swiveled and she grinned evilly. "Say, isn't that Jimmy Mission's Bronco?"

"I think so."

"Oh boy. I should have known. With an ego the size of his, I'm not surprised he needs two parking spaces—oops." They rocked as her car backed into the Bronco's bumper. "I hope I didn't scratch anything."

"The Bronco looks pretty tough."

"I was talking about *my* car." She manuevered forward a few inches. "Now, about you and Tack..."

"I thought we closed this subject."

"*You* did. I was just getting started. Look, Annie. He's good-looking, famous...sort of, in a sports sense, and he obviously wants you. Not to mention, most men wouldn't spend two seconds doing a job if they thought it wasn't going to pay off. If you made it clear to Tack that there was no hope for the two of you and he still went out of his way, that makes him one hell of a nice guy on top of everything. This cowboy's a prize find."

"A temporary find." Thankfully.

"And temporary is exactly up your alley, or so you've said a thousand times. 'I can't take that cowboy home, Deb. This town is too small, I don't want to get serious with anybody, and sleeping with them might give the wrong impression, and what will I say when I have to face Tack and everyone else day after day?' Okay, you had a point, but you won't have to face Tack day after day. Just until he sells or you leave, or both. And nobody will get the wrong impression if the understanding is there right up front. He's leaving. You're leaving. Temporary. Perfect."

Deb was right, Annie thought as she headed up the stairs to the second floor and left her editor examining the rear bumper of her car. Or she would have been if Annie had been telling the truth.

But sex wasn't just sex, not with Tack. She didn't just like the way he made her feel; the way his kisses made her lips tingle or the way his hands drove her mindless with pleasure. She liked *him*. Everything from the deep timbre of his voice, his teasing smiles, the gentle way he cuddled Bones and played with the twins, to the strange light in his eyes when he stared at a Texas sunset as if he'd never really seen one before.

There could never be a temporary for them because Annie felt more for Tack than simply lust. She was falling in love with him again. It was only a matter of time before the emotion consumed her and she forgot all about her future beyond Inspiration. Beyond Tack.

She couldn't, wouldn't do that. No matter how gently he cradled the twins, or kept Annie company, or warmed her from the inside out with his smiles. *Never again.*

TACK CLIMBED onto the dirt bike, flipped the key and gunned the engine. A roar split open the morning silence, deafening even to his own ears that had long ago grown accustomed to the thunderous sound. He killed the engine. Quiet settled in, disrupted only by the distant trickle of creek water, the chirp of birds, the buzz of insects.

He stared at the empty stretch of pasture, drawn by the serene quality. The peace he'd traded for screaming engines and squealing tires and the constant roar of the track. Bitterness swirled inside him and clawed its way up his throat. Years of hard work, of pushing himself to the edge, training until his muscles screamed, and what did he have to show for it?

Trophies. A whole wall of them. So many there were still dozens stuffed away in boxes he hadn't the time or desire to unpack when he'd moved into his house in Encino.

Money. A nice, fat bank account that he rarely touched for anything other than living expenses.

A reputation. He was the best. The top of the game, in his best shape ever. King of the mountain. But for how long? Another race? Another season?

The trophies would tarnish, the money would dwindle. And the reputation would fade when he took a wrong turn, missed a jump or just got slow on his starts.

But this...

Green grass stretched endlessly, giving way to brown hills that jutted upward and kissed a crystal-blue sky.

This went on forever. Tomorrow. Next week. Next year.

The land would still be here, still green and fertile and *home*.

He shook away the thought and gunned the engine again. Kicking the bike into gear, he bolted forward, focusing on the next turn, the next jump, running from the peace and quiet, the memories, the damn present, because Tack had been doing it so long, he didn't know if he could stop. No matter how much he suddenly wanted to.

ANNIE SPENT the rest of the week breaking in the new transmission on her truck, sending out résumés to more newspapers, taking pictures of Echo Canyon and another piece of property Gary commissioned her to shoot, and trying to resist Tack.

Not that he actually did anything to make himself irresistible. True to his word, he didn't touch her again. He simply showed up at her house each evening, freshly showered and ready to help. They talked a little, about people they used to know, Tack's racing and Annie's newspaper aspirations—always keeping the truce and steering clear of the taboo subject of his father. Mostly, however, they worked in companionable silence.

She found herself craving the deep, even sound of his breathing, his footsteps, the feel of his body not far away. It wasn't a sexual feeling but one of security that his presence stirred. She couldn't help remembering the two of them down by the lake, staring at the stars, or in the library, sitting side by side and doing homework. Not talking, just being together. Being friends.

Not friends, she told herself Friday evening as she finished installing the new screen door she'd ordered from Heavenly Hardware. The denial was a vain, last-minute attempt to bolster her defenses, to bury the truth that she'd admitted to herself days ago. That Tack meant more. She felt more. Wanted more—

"Home-repair buddies," she growled. "And that's it."

"Did you say something?" He stood on a stepladder, fixing the sagging porch eave.

Annie's head jerked up and she realized she'd spoken out loud. "I—I asked how the home repair was going, um, buddy?"

"I'm nearly done. How about you?"

"A few more screws and I'm home free." Annie focused her attention on the task at hand.

Tack shifted his stance, fabric brushed fabric as his weight transferred from one leg to another, and a strange sense of peace rolled through her. He was close. *Here.*

She fought back the feeling, tossed her screwdriver into the toolbox with a loud *clang* and blurted out the first thing that came to mind, anything so she didn't have to think about the silence between them, the comfort, and the fact that she'd missed it so much.

"You never did say if you liked my pictures of the ranch?" Annie finished the last adjustment.

"Other than the fact that you didn't deliver them to me personally, they were great." Tack climbed down off the ladder to wipe his hands and sit on the porch steps. "You've got a real eye for landscape."

"Nature offers a lot to the camera." She shrugged. "But the real test is whether or not they'll entice a buyer."

"They don't have to. Jimmy put in a bid a few days ago."

"Already." She busied herself packing up her toolbox. "Looks like things are moving pretty quick." Which meant he would be leaving soon. She forced aside the sudden ache in her chest and smiled. "That's great."

"So you think I should go through with it?"

"If you don't like ranching, selling makes the most sense, and Jimmy is right next door."

"And if I like it?" The question paused her hand in midair. She shot him a sideways glance, but his expression revealed nothing. He simply stared straight ahead at the fast-disappearing sun.

Her breath caught and held. "Do you?"

"Maybe." He shook his head. "Hell, I don't know. It's not as bad as I remember, but it's a lot of hard work."

"That's what Coop always said, but he loved it anyway. He was a cowboy through and through."

"And I'm not." Anger lit his eyes, drew his mouth into a frown.

"Or maybe you're just trying really hard not to be." What the hell was she doing? *Just leave things alone. Let him sell,* cried a small voice inside her. *Tell him what he wants to hear and save yourself.* But at that moment, Annie sensed Tack's fear even more than her own, and she had to say something.

"I know you don't like to talk about Coop." She pushed the toolbox aside, sat down on the steps and motioned to Bones, who flopped down in the space separating them. "But you've got a chip on your shoulder the size of Texas, and avoiding the subject of your father isn't helping anything. Face the past, Tack. Admit that you're still mad at Coop, and giving up the ranch is a way to get back at him. To have the last laugh, so to speak."

"I don't give a damn about revenge."

"You want it so bad, you can taste it." His only reply was a sharp glance. "But there's another part of you that's still holding on," she went on, "the way you were after that homecoming game, mad as anything because Coop had missed it, but still waiting. Still hoping, even though it was over and the stands had cleared, that maybe he might show up. That's why we got together, Tack. Why you were still hanging around when you should have been celebrating the victory with everybody else."

"Leave it alone, Annie."

At the warning note in his voice, it dawned on her that she wouldn't be saying such things to a mere acquaintance, a *buddy*. She wouldn't care enough to ease the hurt.

She did.

The admission fueled her determination. "You told me the other day that your father was too busy for you and your mom. He wasn't, Tack. He was just scared."

"I don't want to talk about this."

"Maybe you don't want to, but you need to, because you don't have a clue what to do with the ranch. You know what your head says, but it's not the same thing you're hearing in here." She tapped her chest. "You're torn. Admit it. Just admit it."

He shrugged. "Christ, Annie, everything's just so damn different. *Everything*, especially you." He spared her a long glance, anger and hurt warring in his blue eyes. "There was a time when you used to be on my side."

The words tugged at the whirlwind of feeling she fought to keep contained. Her throat tightened and her eyes burned. "There are no sides, Tack. Things aren't so different, it's just that we didn't understand them then. I didn't understand my mother and you didn't understand your father. But I stayed and let myself get to know her, and you left. I didn't agree with everything she did, but I finally figured out that it didn't matter. She raised me and loved me even when I was ashamed of who she was. Who I was." While Annie had made peace with her mother, she'd never actually said the words out loud to anyone but Cherry. Until now. "I loved her for that. I *loved* her, and I always will."

He stared at her while she held her breath and waited to see what he would do. Call her a traitor, tell her to shut up, to keep her nose out of his business, his pain.

His gaze finally dropped as he eyed the worn tips of his boots. "What do you think my father was afraid of?"

"Doing the wrong thing. He knew ranching, but he didn't know anything about raising kids, or being a husband. He never had a family, no mother or father, no brothers or sisters. Just the cattle. He knew how to ride shotgun on a herd, to breed the best stock, but that's all he knew."

"So I'm supposed to feel sorry for him? To sympathize?" Tack shook his head as the bitterness welled inside him, making his chest ache, his throat constrict. "How can I when it's his fault my mother died? She was driving *because* of him. She hated to drive. She barely knew how. The only reason she got behind the wheel that night was because she'd promised me. They both had. She and my father were supposed to chaperone the prom, but my father didn't come home as expected. He broke his promise—like he always did—so my mother drove herself." He pushed up from the steps and walked out into the yard, putting his back to Annie as he let the memory take full control. "I thought Coop was there with her that night. I was so busy staring at you, so awed by how you looked in that awful blue dress, I didn't even notice she was alone."

He closed his eyes, remembering the swirls of colored lights, the music, Annie in his arms and the brief glimpse of his mother, lingering near the refreshment table, a smile pasted on her face as if all were right with the world. She'd never shown her emotions, but he'd glimpsed her feelings that night. Not heartache. Love had never figured in with his parents. She'd been angry, embarrassed because her husband was with his mistress. Again. "He should have been there. He should have driven her." His voice broke then and the guilt that had haunted him for too many years poured out. "*I* should have driven her."

"It wasn't your fault, Tack."

Her hand touched his shoulder and every nerve in his body snapped to attention. She was so close, so warm. All he had to do was turn to her, take her the way he'd been wanting to the past few days, but he'd promised himself. And her—especially her.

"Don't do this to yourself," Annie said. "You didn't know. As far as your father goes, you're right. He should have been there, but he wasn't. He made a mistake," she went on. "He made a lot of mistakes, some on purpose, some not, but he still loved you."

Some small part of him wanted to believe, but he tamped the urge down. *No expectations, no hurt.* "You didn't know him."

"I think you're the one who didn't know him," she said. "You're a lot like him. He never liked to talk about the past, either. But there was one night, right after my mother died, when he told me how sorry he was that he'd failed so many people. He did a lot of selfish things, but there was one he regretted more than anything. One he'd do over in a second if he had the chance."

"What?" The word was out before he could stop himself.

"He'd see you play that homecoming game."

The words echoed through his head and something tightened in his chest. But Tack had hated much too long to let go of the feeling now, even if it was eating him alive. "Regret doesn't mean a damn thing. Life doesn't give second chances."

"Doesn't it? You're here. Home. Looks like a second chance to me."

"My father's dead."

"But you're not, Tack. You're the one with the second chance. A chance to make peace with the past, with your father's memory."

"Why don't you leave it alone, Annie? You hated him the same as me back then, and you certainly wouldn't have been caught dead singing his praises. Hell, you barely talked at all."

"I was also a naive teenager. Now I don't bite my tongue for anybody. If there's something that needs to be said, I say it."

"To hell with the consequences?"

"If the stakes are worth it, yes."

"And what are the stakes here?"

"You," Annie finally whispered. "Your peace of mind, your memories. You." Then she walked inside and left him standing alone in the fading sunset.

IT DIDN'T MATTER, Tack told himself as he stood in his father's library and fingered one of the many videocassettes lining the shelves. The tape slid free easily enough, too easy, and Tack's fingers tightened around the black plastic.

So the man had tapes of him. So he'd kept up with races and kept tabs on where his son was living. So he'd actually regretted that one damn football game. So *what?*

It didn't matter. None of it. It was all in the past. Forgotten if not forgiven.

At least that's what he kept telling himself as he sat up the rest of the night and went through the shelves tape by tape, race by race, a bottle of his father's favorite whiskey in his hands. He sat in Coop's chair, the cowboy hat Eli had given him on the desk in front of him, next to the Kawasaki contracts.

Just a signature. That's all he had to give. But every time he picked up the pen, the videotape ended and he had to put another in the machine, or he had to take another drink or adjust the volume on the TV or run his fingers along the brim of that damn Resistol or...*something*. Always something.

He watched the images of himself, and did his best to drink away the ache in his chest. But it lingered until he'd run out of tapes, of Jack Daniel's, and there was nothing to fill the silence but the static from the television and the sound of his own breathing. And the voice.

Ain't nothing more important than this land. Nothing.

Not guilt. Or regret. Or hatred.

Not ten years or thousands of miles.

Not life, or death.

Tack turned toward the portrait of his father, met the intense blue gaze so much like the one he stared at in the mirror every morning.

"You're wrong," he growled, but he didn't feel

the usual bitterness deep in his gut. Just a strange emptiness.

Grief.

"You were *wrong*." The words were softer, directed at his father, at that damn stubborn streak inside of himself that had kept him hating for so long. "But it's okay now."

And as he stretched out on the couch, straw Resistol tipped over his face, and fell into the first real sleep he'd had in days, it *was* okay.

Tack Brandon had finally made peace.

11

"I'VE GOT GOOD NEWS and I've got ridiculous news," Deb said when Annie walked in on Monday morning. "Which do you want first?"

"Give me the ridiculous news."

Deb took a sip from her Bitchiest Babe In Texas mug. "You're working for a wanted woman. Jimmy Mission, the slug, filed charges on me for failure to remain at the scene of an accident and damages to his precious Bronco. A phallic symbol if I ever saw one."

"Failure to remain... Didn't you at least leave him a note?"

"One that specifically told him not to be taking up two parking spaces—I know he did it on purpose—and that he should drive something a bit smaller, to go with the size of his brain and his—"

"You didn't!"

Deb chewed her bottom lip as a rare gleam of uncertainty flashed in her eyes. "You think I went overboard?"

"Don't you?"

"Okay, maybe a teensy bit, but you should have seen his face when he read the note. I was watching from the window. It was priceless."

"Worth a trip to jail?"

"I'm not actually going to jail. Not today. Just

over to the courthouse. The judge will set bail, I'll pay it, then we go to court on Monday. Now, the good news." Deb put down her mug and clasped Annie's hands. "Wally, a drumroll, please." Her excited gaze locked with Annie's. "A certain editor at the *Houston Chronicle* called me less than fifteen minutes ago. They wanted a reference. They're considering you, Annie. For a photographer's position." She smiled. "It's not in the bag, but it's pretty darned close."

Annie tried to grasp the wonderful news. "Me?" Reality sank in and she threw her arms around Deb for a fierce hug. "Oh my God, *me!*"

"That's right. I sent Wally next door to the grocery store earlier to pick this up." She handed Annie a bottle of champagne with a big pink ribbon tied around the neck. "We'll celebrate as soon as I get back."

But by late afternoon, Deb was still tied up in court, haggling with Judge Baines over the bail and the two fines she'd garnered by giving Jimmy Mission a piece of her mind over the entire episode, and Wally had left for an evening class at the college.

Annie grabbed the champagne, her purse and camera bag, and headed home. She pulled into the driveway, killed the engine and simply sat there, listening to the *knock-knock* as the engine sputtered then quieted. Her gaze hooked on the lifeless house and, for the first time, Annie dreaded going inside. Even the puppies weren't there. Deb had borrowed them to scare off the neighborhood cats that were trashing her garden.

Alone.

She was still sitting there, staring straight
ahead when Tack pulled into the driveway and
parked beside her.

He wore a faded denim work shirt, jeans and
scuffed black boots. A day's growth of beard
crept down his strong jaw. Fierce blue eyes
caught and held hers as he climbed off the bike
and walked the few feet to her.

"Did you just get here?"

"Actually," she admitted, "I've been here for a
while."

"Care to tell me why you haven't gone inside?"

"Not really." She traded her unsettling
thoughts for a smile. "One of the newspapers I
applied to is interested in me."

"That's great, Annie."

"Deb and I were going to celebrate, but she's
busy. I'm doing some commission work for Gary,
so I thought I might take a drive out to Echo
Canyon and catch a few shots of the river while
the sun sets and do a little celebrating of my
own." She stared at the champagne bottle on the
seat next to her, then at him. "You want to come
along?" The words were out before she could
think better of them, not that she would have.

Annie was happy, and she wanted to share that
happiness with someone. No, not just *someone*.
Him.

He grinned, pocketed the keys of his Harley
and rounded the nose of the pickup to climb into
the passenger seat. "I thought you'd never ask."

WHEN THEY REACHED the river, Annie spent the
next half hour snapping pictures of the waning

sunlight and giving Tack a play-by-play description of what she was doing. She talked about everything from the speed of film she used, to adding texture to the photographs by capturing just the right amount of light and shadow.

Tack turned out to be much more interested than she'd ever imagined, and he even took a few pictures of his own. He clicked off some shots of the river, the sunset, her.

"That was great," she said breathlessly, when they finally collapsed on the tailgate of her pickup truck. Dusk settled around them. The radio filtered from the Chevy's cab, filling the growing darkness with a slow country tune.

Tack grabbed the champagne, worked the cork with his pocketknife until it popped. "Now to drink a toast."

Champagne spurted, wetting the front of Annie's blouse and skirt. She laughed and hooked her mouth on the opening to suck up the foaming bubbles. A long, sputtering drink and she passed the bottle to him.

He took a long swallow, his gaze riveted on her face.

Self-consciously, Annie wiped at the wetness on her chin, but Tack reached out and pulled her hand away.

The moment of contact sizzled across her nerve endings and she found herself trapped in the moment.

"Let me." Dark eyes drilled into hers as he waited for her permission, and something shifted deep inside her.

She nodded, expecting a gentle swipe of his fingers.

Instead, Tack leaned in, his tongue flicking out to lap at the champagne on her chin. He didn't kiss her, just licked her skin and nibbled at the corners of her mouth and stirred an ache so fierce she wanted to weep.

"You taste so good, Annie, so damn good."

"It's the champagne."

He pulled away from her to stare deeply into her eyes. "It's *you*."

The words slid into her ears, so soft and low and seductive, and her insides quivered. She fought to remember every reason why she shouldn't want him—that she'd once loved him with all her heart and was in imminent danger of falling hard and fast again. But this...this *heat* flaring between them didn't have anything to do with her heart, or so she told herself.

The truck creaked as Tack got to his feet, stood on the tailgate and reached for her.

"Let's dance, honey."

"Here?" She held out her hand.

"Here." He pulled her upright and drew her a few feet forward until they stood in the middle of the truck bed and faced each other. "Right here," he said, sliding an arm around her waist. "For old time's sake."

It was their first dance all over again. Swaying together in the flatbed of an old pickup truck, the music drifting from the cab. Moonlight filtered through the trees. Celestial shadows danced around them, moving with the faint breeze, lending a dreamy quality to the evening.

A dream. That's what it felt like. As if she were caught in one of her dreams, reliving those few precious hours after the homecoming game when she'd kissed him for the first time.

Her hands crept up the hard wall of his chest, arms twined around his neck and she pressed herself closer. His heart beat against her breasts. His warm breath sent shivers over her earlobe, the slope of her neck. His hands splayed at the base of her spine, his thumb rubbing lazy circles just above the swell of her bottom.

A dream. A sweet, intoxicating dream.

"I want you, Annie. I've never felt this way about any woman before." The words, raw and ragged, shattered the hazy pleasure fogging her senses and jerked her back to reality—to Tack and the all-important fact that he wasn't the young boy who'd swept her off her feet. He was a grown man, harder, hungrier, and Annie was this close to giving in to him.

She tore herself away. Putting her back to him, she stared at the play of moonlight on the water and tried to catch her breath and think. But she couldn't. Her thoughts were focused on the man so close behind her, his presence heating her blood, making the humid air seem hotter, steamier, stealing the air from her frantic lungs.

His words upped the temperature.

"Don't hide from me, Annie."

"I'm not hiding."

"Then look at me, honey, and see how much I want you."

She shook her head.

"Then listen to me," he said, his warm breath

rushing against her earlobe as he leaned in just enough to send goose bumps dancing over her skin, "and hear it."

He took a deep, ragged breath. "You're all I think about, Annie. I close my eyes, and you're there. I open them, and you're there. I used to dream about you, but it goes way beyond that now."

"Don't—"

"I'm not breaking my promise by touching you, but I damn sure won't hide what I feel. You're my fantasy, Annie," he went on. "The only trouble is, you're real. So damn real, and it's taking all I have not to reach for you, to peel your clothes away and see you naked and beautiful in the moonlight." The erotic words slid into her ears to tease her senses and heighten the expectancy pooling inside her. "Your blouse would be the first to go. Then your bra." His voice deepened even further, so husky and arousing. "You have the most incredible breasts. Soft and full with wine-colored nipples that pucker whenever I glance at them." Where he didn't reach out with his hands, he did so with his voice. "Are they puckered now, honey? Tight and hard and sensitive?"

She could barely manage a nod.

"Touch them to make sure."

She wasn't sure why she complied. Maybe it was the moonlight, the soft music, his erotic words or the sheer desperation that overrode the passion in his voice. It didn't matter. While she wouldn't cross the line with him, there seemed nothing wrong with inching toward it. Just a little.

Her fingertip found the tip of her breast. Sensation bolted through her and she gasped.

"So beautiful," he murmured, his lips close to the nape of her neck. Close but not quite there. "Touch the other one, Annie. See if it feels as tight. As needy."

She did. Her fingertips circled the ripe crest until she struggled to draw air into her lungs.

"Do you know what I would do next?"

She knew what she wanted him to do, and it was as if he read her mind, knew her desire as well as he knew his own.

"I would glide my fingertips down your belly real soft and slow."

Her hand followed his instruction, fingertips sliding, searching.

"Like that, baby. Just like that."

Her breath caught when she reached the vee between her legs, her touch burning through the thin material of her skirt and panties.

"Do you like what I'd do to you, honey?" The question rumbled through her head, so deep and intimate, with an undertone of satisfaction and pure male possessiveness.

She nodded.

"Then let me." His voice came out a raw, pained whisper. "Let *me*, Annie. Admit that you feel something for me that you don't feel for any other man."

She was so close to saying the words. Too close.

"It's late." Her shaky voice shattered the spell between them. "I—I really need to get home."

He didn't say a word. He simply jumped down off the tailgate and held out a hand to help her down.

Annie didn't want to touch him. Her control was tentative and she knew a slow, sensuous slide down his hot body would send her over the edge.

She needn't have worried. Hands at her waist, he lifted her to the ground, and promptly let her go.

They drove to her house in silence, with only the wind whistling through the open window. It did little to ease the heat that still raged inside her. Sweat dampened Annie's forehead, slid down her temples. The truck jumped and jolted over bumps. Her sensitive nipples rasped against her bra, her bottom rubbed against the seat. It was only a short ride, but enough to keep her hormones buzzing.

"Just leave the keys under the seat." She practically jumped out of the truck before it rolled to a stop alongside her house. A fraction before she slammed the door, she heard his voice.

"Aren't you tired of fighting, Annie?"

The words followed her to the back door. She knew he wasn't talking about any verbal disagreement, but the need that raged between them. Hunger. She wanted him, and he'd made no secret that he wanted her.

Her hand closed around the doorknob and she paused.

What the hell was she doing?

Reality hit her hard and fast while she stood on her doorstep. Deb must have returned the pups because the twins were barking frantically on the other side of the porch door, while the truck's lights blazed in back of her as Tack waited for her to get safely inside.

He wanted her and she wanted him. *Want.*

It didn't have to go beyond that if she didn't let it, if she cut herself off emotionally from the physical lust and kept her emotions carefully in check.

Temporary.

It was only a little while. Annie could guard her heart for the next few days and enjoy herself in the process. Couldn't she?

She could.

She *would*.

She desperately wanted another memory to add to her store, another sweet dream to comfort her in her lonely future, because she knew, no matter where her dreams led her, she would never find another man like Tack.

Her fingers abandoned the doorknob and she turned. The side of the house to her left blocked her from Mrs. Pope's prying eyes, while an endless field stretched to her right, the garage at her back. Plenty of seclusion for what she had in mind.

The headlights blazed, blinding her and obliterating everything beyond the beams, including the darkened cab where he sat, but Annie didn't care. He could see her and that was all that mattered.

Leaving her purse at the back door, she stepped down off the steps and stood in the shower of headlights.

Yes, she was tired of fighting.

Tired of losing.

For once, Annie wanted to taste victory, however brief.

She took a deep breath, gathered her courage and slid the first button of her blouse free. The material soon parted and slid down her arms. Trembling fingers worked at the catch of her bra, freeing her straining breasts. The scrap of lace landed at her feet. The gauzy material of her skirt joined the growing heap until Annie stood in nothing but her panties and a slick layer of perspiration. She hooked her thumbs at the waistband, slid them down and stepped free.

Her first instinct was to cover herself, but she fought it, determined to show Tack just how much she wanted him.

Tack.

She focused on the image of him in her mind, not the boy from years past, but the man who smiled and teased and made her feel beautiful and wicked and wanted.

The warm night air whispered over her bare shoulders and breasts. Her nipples tightened, throbbed, but she touched herself just to be sure.

Just for him.

Her breath caught at the first swirl of fingertips at the aching tips. She wanted to close her eyes, but she forced them open, kept them trained straight ahead just at a point above one of the beams where she knew he sat. Watching.

Her hands moved lower, down the slick, quivering skin of her stomach, to the damp curls at the base of her thighs. The air seemed to stand still around her. Even the twins' harsh barks faded for a few heartbeats. Her breath caught, and she touched herself. One fingertip slid along the soft, wet folds between her legs, heat pulsed through her hot body and a shameless moan curled up her throat.

The engine died and the headlights flicked off, plunging Annie into a blinding darkness. A door slammed. Boots crunched across the gravel.

She barely managed to blink before he reached her. He stopped, paused, waiting for her to say the words and she did.

"You aren't any man, Tack. I want you. *You.* I have for the past ten years, and now it's even more intense because you aren't a figment of my dreams or wishful thinking. You're flesh and blood and you want me back."

Strong, muscled arms wrapped around her and drew her close as his mouth captured hers in a deep, thorough kiss that sucked the air from her lungs and made her legs tremble.

Annie clutched at his shoulders. Denim rasped her sensitive breasts and thighs in a delicious friction that made her quiver and pant and claw at the hard muscles of his arms.

Strong hands slid down her back, cupped her bottom and urged her legs up on either side of him. Then he lifted her, cradled and kneaded her buttocks as she wrapped her legs around his waist and settled over the straining bulge in his jeans.

"Please," she whimpered, rubbing herself against him.

As anxious as Tack was to be inside the warm, sweet woman in his arms, he'd waited too long to have it over with at the flick of a zipper and the hard thrust of his thighs, and that's all it would take.

He stilled her movements and rested his forehead against hers long enough to drag some air into his lungs and give his fogged brain a burst of much-needed oxygen.

"Not here, Annie. Not like this." He leaned behind her, opened the back door and manuevered his way across the fenced-in porch, Tex and Rex snapping at his heels. Blackness engulfed them as he stepped inside the kitchen and inched the door closed behind him, leaving the two excited puppies on the porch.

He carried her to the bedroom, stretched her out on the bed and flipped on the bedside lamp.

"Here," he said, leaning back to stare into her eyes for a long moment. "Like this."

And then he kissed her, long and slow and deep. His tongue tangled with hers, stroking, coaxing until she whimpered and tugged at the waistband of his jeans.

He covered her hand and stilled his movements. "If I take them off, there's no way this is going to go slow, and I want it slow between us. The first time, your first time, I was an anxious kid..." He drew in a deep, shuddering breath. "And my first night back in town, I was drunk. Both times I was thinking about me, Annie. About how you made me feel, how desperate I was to be inside you. But I want to make you feel this time. That's all I've been thinking about. How I'd touch you, what I'd do..."

"So stop thinking and do it."

He grinned at her impatience and feathered his lips over hers, so light and teasing it drew a frustrated moan from her. Then he licked a path down her fragrant neck, the slope of her breast, before pulling back to stare at her. "You're so damn perfect, Annie." His tongue flicked out, lapped at the tight nipple like a cat tasting sweet cream.

Her fingers threaded through his hair and held him to her breast as he suckled her until she writhed beneath him, her hips moving, begging for more. For him.

The blood rushed through his veins, his erection pressed painfully against his jeans, desperate for release, but he held himself in check, determined to take his own pleasure by pleasuring her.

He nibbled a path down the warm skin of her belly to the damp curls between her legs. His fingertips trailed reverently over her slick feminine folds and she gasped.

"Ah, honey, you feel so good. So hot and wet... Just the way I want you."

His hands touched the insides of her soft thighs, spread her legs until she was wide-open for him. He cupped her bottom and tilted her closer. At the first glide of his tongue, she bucked. A strangled cry burst from her lips.

"Shhh," he murmured, fingers stroking, soothing.

"It's just—" she gulped for air "—no one's ever done that. I wasn't expecting..." The words tangled in a sob.

"Don't expect, Annie. Just relax and feel. That's all you have to do, baby. Just feel."

When he touched her with his mouth, she started, but gradually her muscles relaxed. Her legs spread wider, giving him better access to the sweetness deep inside. He feasted on her, his tongue rasping the tender flesh until she threaded her fingers through his hair, arched her hips and shuddered with the force of her release.

Several frantic breaths later, Tack slid up her sweat-dampened body and stretched out on his side to look at her.

Her silver hair lay spread out on the pillow, several damp strands clinging to her flushed face. Her eyes were closed, her full lips parted in breathless rapture. He'd never seen a woman look so beautiful, so sexy, so...*real.*

Tack didn't count on the sucker punch to his gut just the sight of her caused. Nor did he count on the way her soft sigh echoed in his head and made his blood thrum and his heart miss its next beat. And no way in hell did he count on the fierce wave of possessiveness that swept through him. The sudden, desperate urge to brand every inch of her as his and touch her in ways no man could.

Ways no man ever would because Annie Divine was his.

Whether she admitted it or not.

Then her green eyes opened, her hands reached out, stroked the rock-hard length of him through his jeans, and all thought fled. His eyes closed and he relished her touch all of five hearbeats before he caught her hand.

"If you don't stop, I'm liable to explode."

"That's the idea."

"Not yet. There are a few more things I want to do to you."

"Actually," she purred, "there are a few things *I* want to do to *you*. You aren't the only one who's been fantasizing."

Annie unbuttoned his jeans, slid the zipper down and he sprang hot and huge and throbbing into her hands. Her fingertips stroked the long, solid length of him and a pearl of liquid beaded on the plum-ripe head. Annie smiled, dipped her head and demonstrated one of her favorite fantasies.

She tasted his essence, loved him with her mouth as he splayed his fingers through her hair and cradled her head. She pleasured him until his chest pumped from his frantic breathing and his fingers clenched into fists.

"Stop!" he gasped, and she did, because as much as she wanted to please him, she wanted him deep, deep inside her even more.

He shed his jeans and settled between her legs, his weight pressing her back into the mattress. His erection slid along her damp flesh, making her shudder and moan and arch toward him, but he held back.

"Are you still on the Pill?" he asked, remembering what she'd told him the morning after his first night back.

"Yes." He pressed just a fraction into her and she trembled. "And—" she caught her bottom lip as he slid a fraction more "— there's no chance of your, um…*it* shriveling up and falling off—" The words caught on another tremble. "You asked me once before about past lovers, but I don't have any." Her gaze caught his. "There's only been you, Tack. Just you." She wasn't sure what prompted the admission, only that she wanted him to know. Tonight, she'd vowed to put her fears and doubts on hold and enjoy every moment in his arms.

Tonight.

His expression grew serious and his eyes brightened to a feverish blue. "There's never been anyone but you," he told her. When she started to protest, he slid just an inch into her and the words caught on her lips.

"In my head and my heart," he added, making her want him all the more for his honesty and the heartfelt sincerity gleaming in his eyes. "Only and always you, Annie."

And then he plunged fast and sure and deep, burying himself to the hilt in one luscious thrust that tore a joyful cry from her lungs.

"Wrap your legs around me, honey, and hold on."

She did, the motion lifting her body. He slid deeper, the sensation of being stretched, filled, consumed by the raw strength of him stealing her breath for several long moments.

He started to move, building the pressure, pushing them both higher, higher until they reached the top of the mountain and teetered on the edge. With one final thrust, he pumped into her and sent them both over.

Annie cried out his name, her nails digging into the hard muscles of his shoulders, her legs clamping tight as her body milked him of every hot, sweet drop of his release.

When he rolled over without breaking their intimate contact and cradled her on his chest, Annie felt such pure joy that it frightened her.

She fought the feeling back down, consoling herself with the fact that he would be gone soon. She didn't have to worry about making the same mistake as her mother and sacrificing her future for a man, because she and Tack had only tonight. Now.

Annie held the knowledge close and fixed her attention on the steady thud of his heart, the strong arms around her, the chest hairs tickling her cheek.

This moment.

12

"THIS HEAT is killing me." Moonlight filtered through the bedroom window along with a slight breeze that provided little relief to Annie's sweat-drenched body. She wiped the moisture from her face and took a long drink of the iced tea she'd retrieved from the kitchen.

She felt his smile even before she saw it, a warmth stealing through her insides followed by a slash of dazzling white as he loomed over her. His gaze locked with hers and the expression faded.

"Let's see what I can do to help." He took the glass from her hands, his fingertips brushing one already sensitive nipple. She caught her bottom lip as electricity tingled up her spine.

Condensation dripped onto her stomach, sliding over her feverish skin as Tack brought the glass to his lips. He took a long drink of tea and caught an ice cube between his teeth.

Annie's body arched toward him as he touched the ice to her throat. The mixture of hot, hungry lips surrounding shivering relief, sent a jolt of electricity through her and she gasped.

He worked his way down, sliding the ice over her feverish skin. At the first touch to her nipple, a sob caught in her throat. The touch was hot and cold, the sensation both pleasure and delicious pain as he circled the throbbing peak.

Then the sensation disappeared. Her eyes opened in time to see him tip the glass. Cold liquid dribbled onto her belly and she gasped.

"You'll get me all sticky and wet."

"Mmm," he murmured as he surveyed his handiwork. "Sticky and wet." His fingers slid down to probe the drenched flesh between her legs for emphasis. "Just the way I like you."

He pressed a finger deep, deep inside her and lapped at the sweet tea on her belly.

Annie gasped at the rasping heat of his tongue, the cold dribble of tea, the pressure of his wonderful fingers working her into a frenzy. The ripe smell of sweetness and sex and hungry male filled her nostrils, arousing her senses the way Tack aroused her body.

Another cold dribble and she caught her bottom lip to keep from screaming from the delicious sensation.

"I didn't realize I was so thirsty," he murmured against her quivering belly.

"You're going to ruin the sheets," she said in a shaky voice as he dribbled another trickle across her scorching skin.

"I'll buy you new ones." His movements stilled as he leaned up to stare at her. "If you say it's okay, Annie. Only if you say it's okay."

He would never know how much the words meant to her, how they slid into her ears and sent a sweet warmth spreading through her more fierce than the physical response his touch drew.

Because she knew then that he respected her independence, her control.

A smile tugged at her lips as she traced the curve of his stubbled jaw. "Fast and wild," she said, reaching down his sweat-slick body to stroke his rigid sex. Her fingers wrapped around him and a fierce light flared in his eyes. "We had it slow and sweet, now I want it fast and wild." She rolled him over and straddled him.

Her stare never shifted from his as she impaled herself on his hard, hot length in one exquisite motion that took both their breaths away.

He gripped her hips to set the pace, but she caught his hands and urged them to the bed. As if he sensed her need to call the shots, to drive them both to the brink of madness and relish the feminine power she held over him, he followed her command. Tanned fingers gripped her sheets.

"Just sit back and enjoy the trip," she whispered before capturing his lips in a deep, erotic kiss that sent a shiver through his hard body.

And then she started to ride him, fast and wild, until she brought them both to a shattering climax and they collapsed together, hot and spent and sated.

For the moment.

Annie woke the next morning to find the sheets tangled and the bed empty. Panic gripped her, a sudden feeling of emptiness that made her heart pound faster, until she heard the slow drawl of his voice from outside. She climbed from the bed, pulled on a pair of shorts and a tank top, and walked out onto the front porch to see Tack standing in her front yard wearing nothing but his jeans and a grin.

"Walking around half-naked," Mrs. Pope huffed from her flower garden. "What's the neighborhood coming to?"

"Come on, now, Earline. You were catching a peek and checking me out when I bent over." He winked and Mrs. Pope turned a bright shade of pink. "Admit it, darlin'."

"I was doing no such thing. I'll have you know I'm a God-fearing Christian woman and I have better things to do with my time than stare at a half-dressed man who parades around with his pants unbuttoned without an ounce of decency."

He gave her a knowing smile. "And how would *you* know if you weren't checking my... *decency* out?"

Mrs. Pope fired an even brighter shade, and Annie couldn't help herself. Maybe it was the past night of wondrous lovemaking, but she was feeling charitable. "Tack, come back inside and stop bothering Mrs. Pope. She's got roses to tend."

Mrs. Pope's head snapped up and her gaze locked with Annie's. "It's all your fault." She jabbed her gardening spade in Annie's direction. "You're the heathen giving this neighborhood a bad name. Leaving your lights on at all hours, letting those mongrel pups run wild, bringing home half-naked men."

The words prodded old wounds and reminded her of so many similar scenes, only the accusations had been directed at her mother. While Cherry had been in love, she'd never been proud of being the other woman, and so she'd let people talk. She'd done her penance by hanging her head and shying away from confrontation because she'd felt deserving of the gossip.

Like mother, like daughter.

Annie summoned her courage, stepped down off the porch and walked over to Tack.

"Just one man," she told Mrs. Pope. "This man, not that it's any of your business. What I do, who I do it with—none of it is your business, Mrs. Pope." And then she kissed him, in front of God and Mrs. Pope and anyone who might have driven by.

"Are you all right?" he asked when Mrs. Pope had walked into her house and slammed the door.

She nodded and smiled. "A little tired and very hungry."

He slid an arm around her waist and steered her toward the house. "I'll make you breakfast. I cook great pancakes."

"Actually," she said, a wicked gleam in her eyes, "I had something a little different in mind. I've got a sudden craving for peaches."

IT WAS the most tiring weekend of Annie's life, and the most incredible. She spent Saturday and Sunday working on the sales shots for Echo Canyon with Tack taking a break from the ranch to act as her assistant. He carried her equipment and followed her around, and made love to her. In the sweet grass with the sun shining down on them. In the cool river with the moonlight playing off the surface and the stars blazing overhead. In the hot, blistering heat of her bedroom.

It was incredible, unforgettable, and it was almost over.

Thankfully. The loving was too fierce, the joy too consuming, the need growing with every moment she spent with him.

She forced the thoughts away and concentrated on going over this week's schedule. Only a few more days. She could hold out until then, keep her emotions in check. She could.

"Somebody had a good weekend," Deb chimed as she walked by Annie's desk. "My sources have it that you and Tack were seen together several times driving around town. Is it safe to assume you and this cowboy are an item?"

Annie smiled despite herself. "A temporary item."

Deb gave her a thumbs-up then sank onto the corner of the desk. She sighed. "It's good to know somebody's life is looking up. Mine stinks. The trial is today. Speaking of which," she glanced at her watch, "I need you to hold down the fort for a little while."

"I could hold down the fort," Wally grumbled from the corner. "If somebody around here would just give me a break."

Deb and Annie exchanged amused glances.

"So, can you?" Deb asked Annie.

"No problem. I don't have another assignment until after lunch..." Her words faded as a familiar sensation skittered over her senses.

She turned to find Tack standing in the doorway, looking tired and worn and happier than she'd ever seen him.

Just the way she felt.

"I came by to see if you're free for lunch?" he explained.

"I would love to, but I promised Deb—"

"She's definitely free," Deb cut in. She dropped a huge key ring on Wally's desk. "Heads up, Ace. You just got lucky." While the copy boy stared at the keys as if he were holding a winning lottery ticket, Deb turned to Annie. "Wally's in charge for the next few hours. Don't ever let it be said that Deb Strickland stood in the way of true lust!"

A HALF HOUR LATER, after following Tack out to the Big B, Annie stood in the wildflower field near her mother's headstone and stared at the newly erected stone bench.

"What is this?" she asked.

"It's a bench."

"I know that, but why?"

"I thought you might like to come out here and sit sometimes. Do you like it?"

"Yes." She blinked back the tears that threatened to overwhelm her.

A bribe. That's what she wanted to think, but this wasn't a dozen roses or a box of chocolates or an expensive trinket, or any of the other things Coop had used to win her mother's favor and bend her to his will.

This was…*different.*

"I was never really close to my mother," he went on in a quiet, strained voice, as if the words fought to get out just as he battled to hold them back. "In a lot of ways, she was like Coop—quiet, reserved, fixated on the ranch. That's why my father's affair never bothered her half as much as it bothered me. She married this ranch, not him."

"I still don't understand why you did this. You never liked my mother."

"I never liked that my father liked her. I never really knew her enough to say one way or another. Never even said hello."

"What are you trying to say?"

"That maybe I should have. Maybe I should have given her a chance. Given my father a chance... Hell, I don't know. It doesn't matter anyhow. What's past is past and I can't change anything. I just wanted you to know that I'm glad for you, Annie. I'm glad you made peace with her." His words rang with sincerity and a tremble echoed in Annie's heart. "I didn't want to be, but I am."

She sank onto the bench and trailed her hand over the smooth stone, but she didn't feel stone. She felt Tack. His pain. His peace. She *felt* him the way she had so long ago. Despite her best efforts, she was falling for him all over again.

"Truth or dare," she finally said. "I pick truth." She stared at the headstone glittering in the mid-morning sun, keenly aware of him so close. His heat, his strength, the frantic *bam, bam* of her own heart. "I spent my whole life trying to prove to myself and everyone else that I was nothing like my mother. She was outgoing, beautiful, flirtatious, so I made sure I was just the opposite. Then you came along and I realized I was more like her than I ever thought."

"I don't understand."

"You made me feel things, Tack. You stirred a passion I'd convinced myself I didn't possess—a passion my mother was notorious for. When you left, I wanted to hate you, to forget you, but I couldn't. Just like my mother couldn't hate or forget your father or shut him out of her life. That's what changed our relationship and drew us together. Not her illness, but the fact that we cared about two men we could never, ever have."

"I didn't mean to hurt you, Annie. I had to leave."

"I know that, and I'm glad. I always knew that love between two people didn't guarantee a happy ending. My mother was living proof that love is more pain than pleasure. Some people aren't meant to be together. My mother and your father were two of them. You and me…we weren't meant to be together either." She shook her head. "Your leaving was for the best. I realized then that loving someone else wasn't half as important as loving myself. I learned to make my own way and my own happiness."

"I'm signing the final sale papers today."

"That's great."

"I have to leave," he added, as if he meant to convince her, but Annie didn't need any more proof than the strange fluttering in her stomach, the sudden ache in her chest as her heart admitted what her mind wasn't yet prepared to accept.

There was no falling involved. Annie was in love with him.

"I *have* to…" His voice faded into a heated

curse. Then Tack Brandon did what he did best.

He walked away.

HE WASN'T STAYING.

Tack headed back to the house to meet Gary and get on with things. The sale, and the Kawasaki contracts he'd been avoiding much too long.

No, he wasn't staying. No matter how much Tack had come to like the feel of a horse beneath him during the day, a clear blanket of stars overhead at night. No matter how fond he'd grown of Bones, or how he liked watching the sun set from Annie's front porch.

Or how much he liked watching Annie, talking to her, being with her. No matter how much he wanted to prove her wrong.

Love.

What did he really know about love?

He didn't. He'd grown up in a household devoid of love, and while his mother had cared for him, she'd never been affectionate, and his father...

Tack didn't know anything about love.

He only knew that hearing the tears in Annie's voice had twisted a knife in his chest, listening to her confess she'd loved him once had sent a burst of joy through him, and seeing the gratitude in her eyes when she'd touched the bench so lovingly had filled him with satisfaction. Pride. Happiness.

Love.

Dammit, he couldn't stay. He was a motocross racer, not a cowboy. He lived for the thrill of the race, the wind rushing at his face during a good ride, the sweat gliding down his temples, the

aches and pains from taking too many turns and a
rough ride that made him feel tired and worn and
sore and so damn good because he'd accom-
plished something very few people ever did.

"He's down!"

The cry cut into Tack's thoughts and he picked
up his steps, aiming for the corral instead of the
ranch house. He reached the fence just in time to
see Fern rear up on her hind legs. Two cowboys
desperately tried to anchor her with ropes, while
a handful of men helped a wounded Eli from the
corral.

"What the hell happened?" Tack met Eli at the
gate.

"Tried to saddle her today. She kicked and
snapped my arm clear in two."

"You boys get the truck and get him to the hospital," Tack ordered, sending two hands scurry-
ing toward the garage and another to fetch Vera.

"Had to give it one last shot," Eli said, "for
Coop's sake. Thought I had her, too." He groaned
as Tack examined the foreman's twisted arm. "As
smart as she is, you'd think she'd realize breaking's for her own good. She ain't no use like she is,
wild as all get-out. No good to anybody."

The words rang in Tack's ears as Eli left with
two cowboys and a worried Vera, headed for
Grant County Hospital.

No good to anybody.

He watched as the cowboys loosened the ropes
and hightailed it out of the corral before Fern
could do some damage to them. The horse
danced a few seconds, before settling down.
Calm. As calm as the quarter horses in the adjoin-

ing stable. But it was just a front for the light that glittered in her eyes.

"Tack, you ready?" Gary shouted from the back porch of the house. "We're meeting Jimmy in a half hour."

"I'll be right there."

His gaze swiveled back to the animal, to the gleam in her eyes, the wildness.

He recognized it because he saw it in his own eyes when he looked in the mirror. Smelled it in the fine scent of leather and tobacco and fear when he sat in his father's study and tried to concentrate on the books—the walls and the memories closing in on him. Felt it deep in his bones when anybody—Eli or Annie or even Bones—got too close and made him think beyond racing and winning.

The truth hit him then as he stood there, staring at the horse. At himself. It wasn't the ranch he'd always hated, the cowboying, it was his father's pushing it on him. The way Eli had tried to push the saddle onto Fern's back.

Truthfully, Tack liked cowboying. He enjoyed the feel of the horse beneath him, the bone-tiring work that made him feel worn and sore and so damn good because he was doing something that mattered. Caring for the horses, the stock, the land.

Hell, he loved it. Not because he had to, because it was his duty or his legacy or his job, just *because.*

Things were different now. Tack had a choice. And he was staying.

"DON'T TELL ME," Deb said as she watched Annie slide the phone into place. "It was the *Houston Chronicle*." At Annie's nod, she squealed, "You got it, didn't you?"

Annie replayed the phone conversation in her head and wondered why she didn't feel near the excitement she'd anticipated just a few days ago.

We want you, Miss Divine. Your work is good and we'd like to offer you a position on our staff.

"Yes."

"I knew it!" Deb clapped her hands. "Photographer?"

Annie nodded again. "They want me to start next Monday."

"Monday!" Deb squealed, before the news sank in and her smile disappeared. "Monday. But that's only a week away."

"I know it's short notice." She had eight days to pack up everything she owned and find a place in Houston. "I could call them back and ask for more time."

"You'll do no such thing. It's just…" She raised suddenly misty eyes to Annie. "I'm going to miss you."

"I know." Annie wrapped her arms around the woman and they hugged.

Wally walked in, Annie filled him in on the news, and he joined the hug.

Deb finally sniffled and pulled away. "I hope nobody sees this. It'll ruin my image."

"I've seen it," Wally informed her. "Prime blackmail material."

"You'd blackmail the woman giving you a promotion?"

"A promotion?" His eyes widened with excitement.

"I need somebody to help me fill Annie's shoes, not that you could even come close. But you're a hard worker."

"Yeeeee-hahhhhhhh!" He grabbed Deb around the waist and twirled her for a long moment, before she threatened bodily injury.

After he plopped her on her feet, Deb pulled and tugged at her red suit. "Now, if we've got all this emotional stuff over with, I say let's hit BJ's. We've got a lot to celebrate. Annie's job, Wally's new promotion and my new lease on life."

"Which is?" Annie asked.

"To make Jimmy Mission as miserable as is humanly possible. The slug won in court. I have to pay him damages."

"That seems fair considering you caused the damages," Annie said.

"And pain and suffering he endured while driving around with red paint smeared on his bumper."

"That's ridiculous."

"That's exactly what I said." At Annie's raised eyebrow, Deb shrugged. "Okay, I said that and a few more choice things that got me another nice, big fat fine for contempt." She blew out a deep breath. "Let's go, gang. I'm buying."

A HALF HOUR LATER, Deb was on her fourth drink while Annie worked on her second and Wally twirled Jenny Peters around a crowded dance floor.

"Monday," Deb mused. "Don't get me wrong.

I'm thrilled for you, Annie. You know I am. It's just that I was kind of hoping you might end up staying here. Maybe freelance for magazines, open a photograpy studio, do calendars or brochures or anything that lets you showcase your work, and do it right here.''

"I've got too much invested in my career to up and change now." Annie had spent too many years focusing herself, working toward a specific career goal, to suddenly switch courses. She had a journalism degree, after all. Years of experience in the field. Stay here and do straight photography? *No.*

No matter how appealing the idea or how much she'd been enjoying the landscape shots she'd been doing for Gary, or how many of the same thoughts she'd been having lately, especially since Tack had rolled back into town.

She had to finish what she'd set out to do.

She downed the last of her drink and steeled herself. "I knew there was someone out there who wanted me."

"Ditto on that, honey." Deb chuckled. "And he's walking this way.''

Annie's gaze swiveled just in time to see a pair of worn jeans moving toward her. Her gaze slid higher, over trim thighs and a lean waist, to a faded denim shirt covering a broad chest... *Tack.* A straw Resistol sat atop his dark head, slanted at just the angle she remembered and making him look every bit the cowboy he was trying so hard not to be.

Boy? No, he was every bit a man, and Annie was all too aware of that fact, of the man's hunger that burned in his gaze when he looked at her the way he was right now.

"What brings you here?" she asked as he stopped next to her table, Jimmy Mission at his side.

"Celebrating," Jimmy replied, tipping his hat to Annie before flashing a grin at Deb, who scowled.

"You sold the ranch," Annie said.

"Actually—" Tack's gaze caught and held hers "—I didn't. That's what we're celebrating. That and Jimmy's win in court. Mind if we join you? There aren't many tables."

"No," Deb said, propping her feet on the chair next to her before Jimmy could sit down.

He frowned. She smirked. Then he leaned over, grabbed her ankles and plopped her feet on the floor, before sliding into the now-vacant seat.

"Pain and suffering for a little bumper scratch," Deb muttered. "That's the stupidest thing I've ever heard."

"No, the stupidest thing was you cussing out the judge," Jimmy replied.

"I hate you."

"Your lips say hate, but your eyes say you want me, darlin'."

"The day the devil starts dishing up snow cones…"

The verbal exchange faded as Annie stared up at Tack, his words echoing in her head like a broken record.

"You really didn't sell?"

He shook his head and the knowledge sank in.

Tack was settling down. Staying at the Big B. Planting roots.

Joy erupted inside her, stirring a wave of panic that made her heart pound faster.

"B-but what about Kawasaki?"

"I tore up the contracts and told them no. I'm retiring."

Her gaze narrowed. "Just like that?"

"Actually, I've been thinking about it for a while, that's why I didn't sign with them right away. I'm tired of being on the road. I need something steady. Besides, Bones has kind of gotten attached to the place, and I've gotten attached to him, among other things." His gaze darkened. "I'm staying, Annie."

"And I'm leaving." Before he could reply, Annie bolted to her feet and fled through the crowd, fear pushing her faster when she heard Tack's shout.

"Annie, wait!"

But she couldn't. He was *staying*. The knowledge sent a wave of panic through her and she picked up her steps. She slammed her palms against the rear exit and stumbled out into the parking lot. Gravel crunched as her legs ate up the distance to her truck.

"Annie!" The name rang out a second before he caught her arm in a firm jerk that brought her whirling around to face him. "Annie, I—"

"Don't say it!" She shook her head, blinking back the tears that suddenly threatened to overwhelm her. "Please don't."

"I love you."

The tears spilled over and she shook her head,

fighting the truth of his words and the emotion in her heart. "Let me go. I—I have to get out of here."

"Annie?" Strong, warm hands cradled her face, his thumbs smoothing her tears. "What is it, baby? Didn't you hear me? I said I love—"

"Don't!" Pleasure rushed through her, so fierce it stirred the fear and the panic and made her fight harder. She pushed at his hands. "Don't make this any harder. Just let me go."

"If saying I love you makes it harder for you to go, then I love you, I love you, *I love you*, dammit!" His eyes took on a determined light. "Because I damn sure don't want you to go anywhere." He gripped her hands with his, ignoring her attempts to pull free. "I thought you felt the same way."

"You thought wrong."

"Did I?" Fierce blue eyes drilled into hers and she came so close to blurting out the truth.

Instead, she shook her head, clinging to her anger and her fear and the pain of hearing her mother cry herself to sleep at night because she'd been so miserable. Because she'd given up everything for the man she loved.

She'd risked it all and she'd gained nothing. Only a lot of pain and loneliness that a few moments of joy couldn't begin to ease.

"I'm leaving, Tack. The *Chronicle* called. I start Monday."

"Houston?" He looked as if she'd landed a punch to his gut. He shook his head. "You can't."

"I *can*. I can do anything I want."

"But I don't want you to go."

"That's just it. It's not about what you want. It's about what *I* want. Don't you understand? I've worked my entire adult life for a chance like this. I can't forget about it now because you say you love me."

"How about because *you* love *me?*"

She shook her head. "It's not enough."

Truthfully, it was too much. The emotion gripping her heart made her want to throw it all to the wind, wrap her arms around him and forget the job, the past, the future—everything but this moment. Now. Him.

No!

"I'm not making the same mistake as my mother." She yanked free and rushed for her truck. Inside, she gunned the engine and took a deep, shaking breath.

Heaven help her, she'd done it. She'd traded Tack for her independence, her pride, her dreams, her sense of self, what her mother had never had the courage, or the desire, to do with Cooper Brandon. So why did it suddenly feel as if Annie had turned her back on the one thing that mattered the most?

Wiping frantically at a flood of hot tears, she chanced a glance in her mirror to see Tack standing where she'd left him, staring after her, fists clenched, his body taut, as if it took all his strength not to go after her.

It was an image that haunted her all through the night and the rest of the week as Annie packed up boxes, made phone calls and prepared for the rest of her life.

Without Tack Brandon.

13

ANNIE RANG Mrs. Pope's doorbell for the third time. She waited a few more seconds then left the envelope she'd been holding on the woman's front step. The drive to Houston was four hours and Annie still had one more stop.

She managed three steps toward her truck before a door opened behind her.

"What's this?"

She turned to find Mrs. Pope staring at the seven dollars stuffed into the envelope.

"The money I owe you."

A strange expression eased the woman's usually hard features. "You're really leaving?"

Annie nodded. "I start my new job first thing in the morning. But don't worry, Gary Tucker said he'll find a nice neighbor for you. He's handling the sale for me. Take care, Mrs. Pope." She turned to walk away, but the woman's voice stopped her.

"You're a good girl, Annie Divine."

Annie turned and stared at the old woman. "What did you say?"

"I said you're a good girl."

It shouldn't matter. It never had. Mrs. Pope had scowled and hollered for most of Annie's life, and it had never mattered. The woman disliked her, and she'd accepted it. Oddly enough, the words warmed Annie's heart anyway.

"I know I razzed you a lot," Mrs. Pope went on, "especially since I retired from the library. I want you to know, though, it isn't because I never liked you. It's just that an old woman like me needs something to keep her going. My Claire's tried to push me into that blasted nursing home over in Grant County for the past ten years. Said I'd have folks my own age to keep me company instead of puttering around here all by my lonesome. What she didn't understand was I had something to do, something pulling me out of bed besides my gardening and Jerry Springer." The old woman smiled. "You called me out on every dadblastit complaint, gave me tit for tat when I got too out of hand. I looked forward to buttin' heads with you, dear. Highlight of my day, and I'm going to miss it. And you. I'm surely enough going to miss you."

Annie wiped at her suddenly misty eyes. "I'm going to miss you, too, Mrs. Pope." And then she turned away because the last thing she wanted to do was cry again. She'd done too much of that over the past week. As she'd packed up the house and said goodbye to all of her friends, more than she'd ever realized she had. Somewhere over the past ten years, as Annie Divine had stopped trying so hard to fit in, she'd done just that. She'd become a part of the town, one of the folks. While there were plenty who didn't like her, there were even more who did.

Granny Baines had baked her farewell cookies and Bobby Jack had given her a goodbye party last night at BJ's. Half the town had come, including Tack. Not that he'd said more than a hello. He'd spent the evening nursing a beer and visiting, but all the while, his gaze had been trained on Annie. As if to say, *Here I am. I've laid my cards on the table. The next move is yours, honey.*

It had surprised her. She'd expected him to come at her like gangbusters, to order and demand and do exactly what his father had done to keep Cherry Divine in town and in his bed.

Tack had done none of that, proving he was less like his father than she'd initially thought.

Not that it mattered. Annie had to leave.

Had? There was no *had* about it. She wanted to leave, to make her own way, to live for herself and no one else for the first time in her life. To make her dreams come true.

If only fulfilling her dreams didn't hurt so damn much.

She steeled herself against the thought and climbed into her Chevy. The puppies sat on the seat next to her in their traveling cage. Annie gave the house one last glimpse, wiped at her watery eyes and pulled out of the driveway for the last time.

"LET HER LOOSE!" Tack yelled, holding on to the reins for all he was worth. The two cowboys holding the ropes on Fern drew them back and she reared up, nearly throwing Tack, who sat firmly in the saddle, riding her for the first time.

He held on, his grip determined as she kicked and stomped and snorted against the feel of the saddle and the weight on her back. Seconds ticked by until she accepted the inevitable and started to calm beneath Tack's guidance.

Cheers went up a few minutes later as he climbed off after a brief, but exhilarating ride.

"That wasn't so bad now, was it, girl?" He stroked Fern's mane. "If only Eli could have been here." But at this moment, his foreman was pacing the hospital, his arm in a cast, waiting for Vera to give birth to their third child. He smiled as he remembered the excitment on Eli's face when one of the boys had come to fetch him from the corral just a few hours ago, yelling, "Daddy, Daddy! It's time!"

Daddy. A pang of envy shot through Tack. While he'd achieved so much in his life, he wanted more.

A home. Kids. *Annie.*

Tack soothed the lathered horseflesh a minute more, gave Fern a final pat and started to unhitch the saddle. He'd just unstrapped the cinch when he caught sight of a familiar white pickup pulling around the house, the truck bed packed full of boxes.

He swung the saddle over the fence post, exited the corral and started toward her. She climbed out of the truck and met him halfway between the house and the barn.

"You're here," he said, his heart revving faster than a primed cycle poised at the starting gate.

"I just wanted to give you something before I left." She handed him a box. "I made it for you. Something to remember me by."

As if he could forget her.

She'd lived and breathed in his memories for so

long, and now she'd taken up permanent residence in his heart, and there wasn't a damn thing he could do about it.

There was, a nagging voice whispered. He could hitch her over his shoulder, take her into the house and love her until she changed her mind. The heat burned so fierce between them, it would be hot enough to change her mind. For a little while anyway.

His fingers itched and he touched her hand. Her gaze met his and he read the fear in her eyes, the expectancy. That's exactly what she expected him to do. What a part of her wanted. That part she was trying so hard to ignore because she was afraid to give up her version of Austin and the Silver Spurs.

She wasn't her mother.

And Tack wasn't his father. He pulled his hand away even though every fiber of him wanted to crush her in his arms and kiss her.

He concentrated on opening the box.

A navy blue photo album lay inside, nestled in tissue paper. Tack pulled the album free and turned to the first page to see several of the panoramic shots Annie had taken of the Big B. He flipped through several more pages, saw more pictures of the ranch, old photos of Tack and his mother, and even one of Annie and Cherry.

"You liked the memory book I made of my mother," she explained. "So I thought I'd make one of Coop."

Tack simply stared and flipped, until he reached the last page that held a full glossy of himself astride a Yamaha race bike, his expression tense as he arched for a jump.

"This was his favorite," she said. "He wrote to your fan club and requested it. If you get lonely for him—"

"When," he cut in. "When I get lonely for him."

She smiled, a beautiful curve to her lips that warmed him even more than the hot Texas sun. "*When*, you can open up the album and you'll be surrounded by all the things he loved. By him."

He swallowed the baseball-size lump in his throat. "Thanks." With stiff fingers, he managed to close the book. His gaze captured hers. "Do you love me? Because if you do, I need to hear it."

Fear brightened her eyes, made her hands tremble and, for a split second he thought she was going to turn and run without ever admitting the truth. To him. To herself.

"Yes."

The word sang through his head, echoed through his heart. He wanted to hear her say it again and again, to feel the one syllable against his lips. "Then stay. We're not Cherry and Coop."

"Don't you see?" Tears filled her voice, betraying the calm she always tried so hard to maintain. "If I stay, we are, Tack. *We are.*"

"Then kiss me, honey. One last time. For old time's sake."

"I don't..." She shook her head, so close to refusing. Then her gaze caught and held his. "For old time's sake." She stepped toward him and touched her mouth to his.

The photo album thudded to the ground. Tack

wrapped his arms around Annie and held her tight, as if he never meant to let go. He gave her a gentle, searing kiss that intensified the ache deep inside him and made him want to hold her forever.

She loved him, he loved her. This was crazy. They could have a life together starting now. *Today.*

A life filled with resentment. While Annie might return his feelings, he knew deep down inside she would always hate herself for not following her ambition, for buckling under the weight of her feelings just as she'd always done in her life.

Maybe she wouldn't. Maybe they'd live happily ever after.

It wasn't a chance he could take. She'd given up so much for the people she cared about, put them and her love for them before her own dreams. As much as Tack wanted her, he didn't want to be another sacrifice.

"I'm not my father, Annie," he murmured against her soft, sweet lips. "And I'm not making the same mistake either." While he knew with dead certainty they were meant for each other, Annie had to discover it for herself.

And if she didn't?

Tack shoved his greatest fear aside and did the hardest thing he'd ever had to do in his life. He let Annie Divine walk away.

"JUST GET THE SHOT and come on, Annie!" David Bruce, the reporter Annie had been assigned to, motioned her toward a beige Infinity. She clicked off two shots of the charity golf tournament winners as they stepped off the podium and rushed to keep up with the man.

Rushed. That described the past three weeks of her life since she'd moved to Houston and started her new job. She'd covered numerous stories and taken an obscene number of pictures, and she couldn't call to mind one single subject. She barely had time to look through her viewfinder before she was hustling off to the next assignment.

Deb had been right. Big-city reporting wasn't what it was cracked up to be, the focus on quantity rather than quality. The reporter told the stories with words while the pictures served only as reinforcement. Inconsequential. A second thought.

"Are you okay?" David asked as Annie climbed into the seat beside him and they swerved out into downtown traffic.

"Fine. A little winded."

"You'll get used to it. This is the major league. Pretty soon you'll thrive on the fast pace."

Annie wasn't placing any bets. While she'd remained true to herself and finished what she'd set out to do—taken the job of her dreams and made the move—her heart was no longer in it.

Her heart was back in Inspiration.

With Tack.

Funny that she'd had to travel hundreds of miles to find the courage to admit that to herself. For the first time in her life, Annie not only understood her mother's choices, she sympathized. Cherry had been caught in a catch-22 situation, stay and be miserable as Coop's mistress or go and be miserable without him.

But Annie's situation had been different.

Had it?

While Tack had mentioned love, he hadn't said anything about marriage or family or a future. Just *stay*.

Maybe he'd wanted nothing more than his father.

Maybe he had wanted more.

We're not Cherry and Coop. Annie forced aside the haunting questions, clipped on her press pass and climbed out when they reached their next stop—the Southwest Bridal Fest, a fashion show and formal-wear convention at Buffalo Bayou Park.

While David interviewed some of the designers, Annie snapped picture after picture of the latest bridal wear, cake creations and floral arrangements. David sought her out twenty minutes later and informed her she had a half hour to catch a bite before they headed over to the Harris County courthouse to cover a charity auction.

The opportunity was too tempting to resist. She left David scarfing down stuffed mushrooms at one of the catering booths and headed toward the trees that lined Buffalo Bayou. She'd been denied the simple pleasure of searching for the right shot, the perfect angle, for weeks now, and she was going into withdrawal.

Which was why she'd made up her mind to change things. She'd sent off a few pictures of the Big B to a Texas magazine and had landed her first freelance assignment.

Aiming her camera, she snapped off several landscape shots, then walked farther away from the crowd, along the grassy, tree-lined bank of the bayou.

She aimed for another picture and a strange awareness skittered over her skin, as if someone watched her.

As if...

She glanced around, her gaze searching the trees behind her. Noise rose in the distance, but Annie was out of eyesight of the festival crowd, with just the trees and the water for company.

It was just her imagination, she finally concluded, turning her attention back to her camera. Because no way in heaven, hell or even Texas could Tack Brandon actually be here—

The thought scattered the minute she sighted the familiar face in her viewfinder.

He'd stepped from behind a nearby tree. The bayou twinkled in the background. The overhead branches swayed with the slight breeze. Sunlight chased shadows across his heavily stubbled face. Her mind flashed back to a similar scene, to a man standing down by the creek bed, eating peaches.

But he wasn't standing. He was walking toward her. And he wasn't eating...

He raised a succulent peach to his mouth, took a bite, and Annie felt the sensation clear to her toes, along with a deep burst of joy in her heart.

"You look like hell," she said as he reached her and she noted the tight lines around his mouth, the shadows beneath his eyes, as if he hadn't slept in days. Weeks.

"And you look like pure heaven, sweetheart." He tossed what was left of his peach.

"What are you doing here?"

Two fingers dived into his jeans pocket and he pulled a familiar scrap of white and peach lace free. He grinned that Texas-heartbreaker grin that made her insides jump as he dangled her panties from one tanned finger. "I thought you might want these back."

A smile tugged at her lips despite her best efforts. "I'm wearing new ones."

Instead of saying, "I'll just keep these then," as he had when they'd played this same scene in the *In Touch* office, he said, "I know, honey. I want those, too."

"So you're here collecting women's lingerie?"

"Just yours, Annie." Desperation flared in his eyes, along with a determination that took her breath away. "Only yours. Always yours. I plan to add every damn pair you possess to my stash because I love you and I'm not letting you go."

She'd been fighting what she felt for him for so long, and her defenses automatically kicked in. "You can't force me to come back."

"I would never do that, and I won't ask you to give up your dreams, either. I've been keeping myself away to let you know I respect your decisions, your ambitions. But I'm here now because I'm following *my* dream. You," he said, his fingertips trailing along her cheek as if he couldn't quite believe she was real. "You're my dream, Annie. I want you. Here, or wherever you go."

"What about the ranch? It's your home."

"You're home." His hands cradled her face, his

thumbs smoothing across her trembling bottom lip. "Wherever you are, that's where I'll hang my hat. Eli knows the Big B like the back of his hand, he'll take care of things as good as I ever could."

"You can't just leave it all, not now that you've made peace and settled things."

"I can, and I will. For you."

"And spend the rest of your life tagging along after me? I don't want that."

Anger flared deep in his eyes as his mouth drew in a grim line. "So you don't love me. Is that what you're trying to say?"

"No! I do love you. With all my heart. It's just…I don't want that." She shook her head and turned to stare at the shimmering creek. Just beyond, the freeway formed a frenzied maze. Cars zipped back and forth, rushing here and there…

This is what she'd traded sun-drenched fields of flowers and picturesque landscapes for. While the city had its own beauty, it didn't hold a permanent place in Annie's heart.

Not like Inspiration.

Home.

Tack.

"One person making all the sacrifices," Annie said. "That's not what love is all about. It's about give-and-take. An equal amount of both."

"Meaning?" He came up behind her, so close she could feel the heat from his body, hear his heart beating in her ears.

Just where Annie wanted him. Now, and forever.

"I proposed an idea called 'Wild About Texas' to *Texas Highways*," she told him. "The idea is for a collection of nature shots showcasing the untamed beauty of Texas. They bought the proposal and asked about making it a monthly feature." She turned and stared into his eyes. "The closest thing to untamed around here is my new next-door neighbor's Doberman. He went crazy when Tex and Rex moved in, and has been trying to have them for lunch ever since."

Hope fired in his deep blue gaze. "Are you saying what I think you're saying?"

"If you think I'm saying I love you and I want to be with you, then yes, I am. On one condition," she said when he started to reach for her. She caught his arms and held him off, determined to resolve the unanswered questions between them. "I'm not my mother. I won't settle for anything less than everything. Love, marriage, babies—*everything*." She swallowed, and forced herself to say the last two words. "Or nothing."

She'd given him the ultimatum, and as much as she wanted to take the words back and accept whatever he offered, she wouldn't. She wanted an equal relationship, mutual love.

He grinned, the sight easing the anxiety that had been coiling inside her. "*Lots* of babies," he declared as he drew her into his arms and hugged her fiercely. "Ten, at least."

"I was thinking two or three," she said, her heart swelling with the certainty that he loved her as much as she loved him.

"Six," he said.

"Four."

"Five and a half."

She drew away, laughter bubbling on her lips. "A half?"

He grinned. "We'll work something out." His expression went from happiness to serious desperation. "Marry me, Annie, and we'll make a home for ourselves at the Big B and have however many kids God blesses us with. You can take pictures to your heart's content and do anything that makes you happy, as long as we're together. I want you in my bed." He touched one nipple and brought the tip to throbbing awareness. "In my heart." His hand slid higher, over the pounding between her breasts. "In my life." His thumb came to rest over the frantic jump of her pulse. "*Everywhere.*"

She smiled through a blurry haze of tears and pulled away from him to grab the hem of her sundress and run her hands up her bare legs.

His expression went from puzzled to hungry. "What are you doing?"

She sniffled and smiled wider. "Giving you a deposit."

She shimmied and wiggled until her peach-colored panties pooled at her ankles. Stepping free, she dangled the scrap of silk in front of him before stuffing the undies into his pocket along with the other pair already in his possession.

"And there will be many more to come. A future of them. *Forever.*" And then she kissed him, surrendering her body to his roaming hands, her heart to his and her soul to whatever the future held.

Love. Happiness. A lifetime of both.

If you enjoyed what you just read,
then we've got an offer you can't resist!

Take 2 bestselling
love stories FREE!
Plus get a FREE surprise gift!

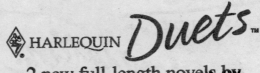

HARLEQUIN *Duets*.™

2 new full-length novels by 2 great authors in 1 book for 1 low price!

Buy any Harlequin Duets™ book and SAVE $1.00!

SAVE $1.00

when you purchase any

HARLEQUIN

Duets.™ book!

Offer valid May 1, 1999, to October 31, 1999.

Retailer: Harlequin Enterprises Ltd. will pay the face value of this coupon plus 8.0¢ if submitted by the customer for this specified product only. Any other use constitutes fraud. Coupon is nonassignable, void if taxed, prohibited or restricted by law. Consumer must pay any government taxes. Valid in U.S. only. Mail to: Harlequin Enterprises Ltd., P.O. Box 880478, El Paso, TX 88588-0478 U.S.A.

Non NCH customers—for reimbursement submit coupons and proofs of sale directly to: Harlequin Enterprises Ltd., Retail Sales Dept., 225 Duncan Mill Rd., Don Mills (Toronto), Ontario, Canada M3B 3K9.

HDUETC-U

HARLEQUIN®
Makes any time special.™

Coupon expires October 31, 1999.

5 65373 00051 9 (8100) 1 06254

Look us up on-line at: http://www.romance.net   HDUETC-U

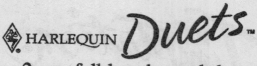

Temptation®

COMING NEXT MONTH

#729 IT TAKES A HERO Gina Wilkins
Bachelor Auction

Romance author Kristin Cole didn't need a man—she needed a hero! With writer's block staring her in the face, Kristin couldn't resist bidding on gorgeous Perry Goodman, just for inspiration. But Perry wasn't a one-night hero. He was holding out for a "happily ever after"—one that included her....

#730 LOGAN'S WAY Lisa Ann Verge

Ambushed! That's how Dr. Logan Macallistair felt when his peaceful retreat was invaded by a sexy redhead. The indomitable Eugenia Van Saun, Ph.D.—botanist with an attitude—was using his cabin for research? He'd been alone and he wanted to stay that way. Still, looking at Ginny, he had a growing appreciation for flowers, the birds and the bees...and who better to explore them with?

#731 NOT IN MY BED! Kate Hoffmann
The Wrong Bed

Carrie Reynolds had only one weakness: Devlin Riley. The sexy adventurer played the starring role in all Carrie's thoughts and fantasies. When Carrie went on vacation, she wasn't particularly surprised that Devlin showed up while she slept, stroking her, seducing her.... Then she woke up—and discovered she wasn't dreaming....

#732 FORBIDDEN Janelle Denison
Blaze

For years Detective Josh Marchiano had been in love with his partner's wife. But now, Paige was a widow—and she was in danger. Torn between guilt and desire, Josh vowed to protect her at all costs. Little did he guess that he'd have to stay by her side all day...and in her bed all night!